HARVEY GIRL

Harvey Girl

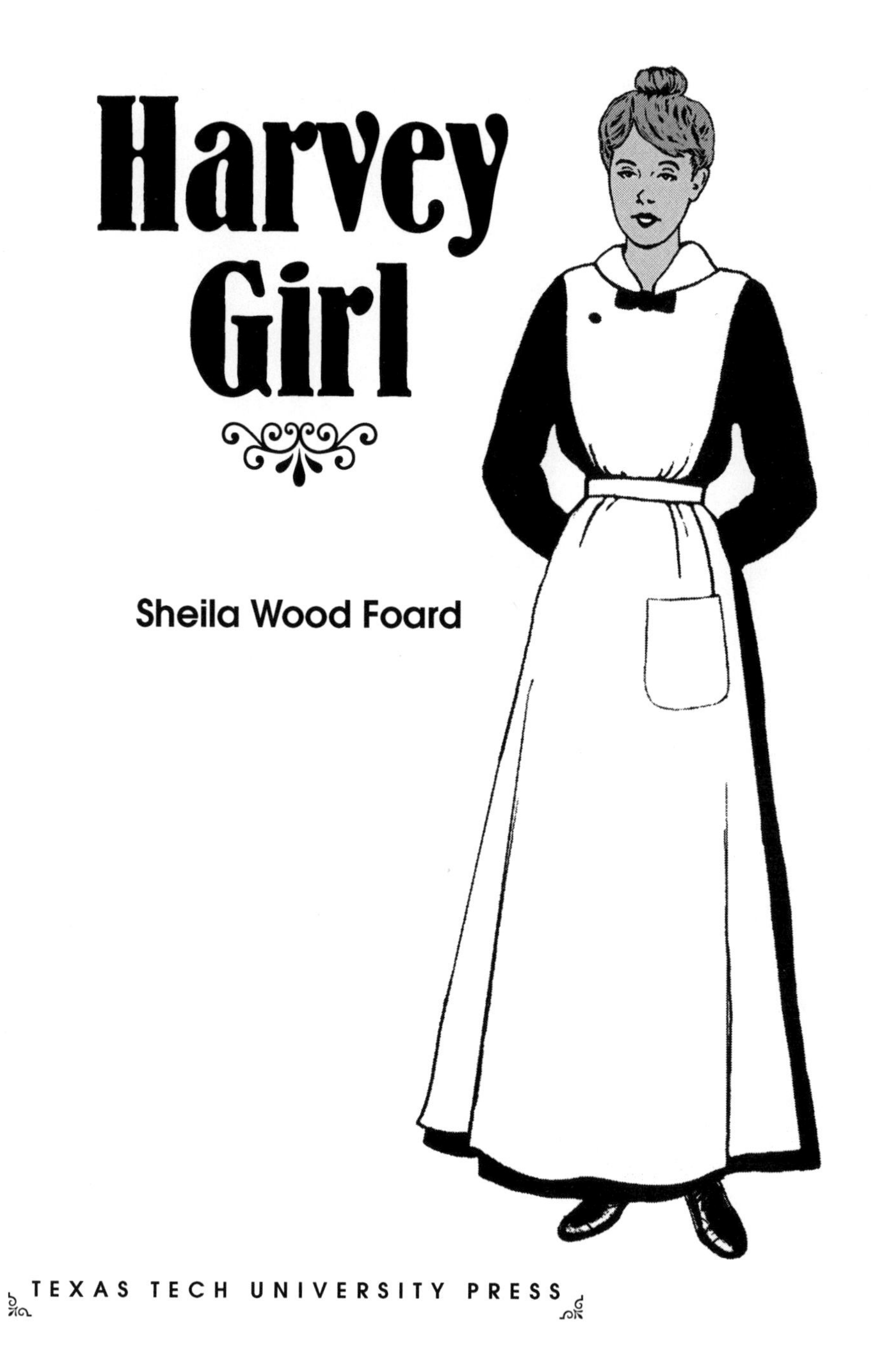

Sheila Wood Foard

TEXAS TECH UNIVERSITY PRESS

This book is typeset in Berkeley. The paper used in this book meets the minimum requirements of ANSI/NISO Z39.48-1992 (R1997). ♾

Designed by Lindsay Starr
Digital cover art based on circa 1915 Brown Photo and Kolb Brothers Photo (both page 150) courtesy of the Grand Canyon National Park Museum Collection.

Library of Congress Cataloging-in-Publication Data
Foard, Sheila Wood.
Harvey Girl / Sheila Wood Foard.
p. cm.
Summary: In 1919, fourteen-year-old Clara Fern Massie runs away from her family's farm in Missouri to earn a living and find adventure as a Harvey Girl, one of the waitresses who worked at Harvey House restaurants along the railroads in the Southwest United States.
ISBN 0-89672-570-7 (hardcover : alk. paper)
[1. Waitresses—Fiction. 2. Self-confidence—Fiction. 3. Runaways—Fiction. 4. New Mexico—History—20th century—Fiction.] I. Title.
PZ7.F72614Har 2006
[Fic]—dc22
2005020220
ISBN-13 978-0-89672-570-6

Printed in the United States of America
12 13 14 15 16 17 18 19 20 / 9 8 7 6 5 4 3 2

Texas Tech University Press
Box 41037
Lubbock, Texas 79409-1037 USA
800.832.4042
ttup@ttu.edu
www.ttupress.org

WITH LOVE AND THANKS

to my husband, Bob,

my son Trae, daughter-in-law Yvonne,

grandchildren Shelby, Virgil,

Melanie, and Jonathan, and

children's writers Kimberley Little

and Linda Herman

Contents

Acknowledgments

Many thanks to all those who have kept the Harvey Girl story alive, especially the Belen Harvey House's docents, Maurine McMillan and Richard Melzer; the Slaton Railroad Heritage Association, Tony Privett, and Tex Wilson; Grand Canyon National Park's Museum Collection staff and all its interpreters; Ozark National Scenic Riverways, its superintendent, Noel Poe, and its interpreters; Polly Welts Kaufman, author of *National Parks and the Woman's Voice; Kansas City Star* columnist Marli Murphy, my "tour guide" at Kansas City Union Station; and all the former Harvey Girls and Fred Harvey Company or Atchison, Topeka, and Santa Fe Railway employees, who have shared their experiences with me in person or in print.

HARVEY GIRL

1

Gettin' Above Your Raisin'

Not long before I ran away from home, Miss Forester told us scholars in Chubb Hollow School that women in America might soon be able to vote.

I sat spellbound, listening to her tell the story of our country's army of suffragists. But I heard a boy behind me whisper, "What the heck's a suffra-just? Is it scary as a gowrow?" Then he snickered.

Miss Forester didn't answer him. I guess she figured everybody knows suffragists are women who have fought for years to get voting rights so they can have a say in how our government is run, same as men.

And a gowrow is a big old lizard—twenty foot long—with huge tusks. Old-timers spin yarns about gowrows that live in Ozark caves and steal calves to eat. They're hatched from soft-shelled eggs as large as washtubs and carry their young in a pouch like a possum.

Miss Forester went right on with her lesson. "At long last, Congress has passed the Nineteenth Amendment. Now the suffragists are fighting to get the amendment ratified so it will become law. Our state has voted for ratification. We should be proud to live in Missouri."

We girls in the one-room school applauded. The boys whistled, but I knew some of them, like my bratty little brother, just wanted to see who could make the most noise. To me the suffragists' story was more exciting than the ones told about the heroic deeds of Teddy Roosevelt. This story was about Susan B. Anthony, Elizabeth Cady Stanton, Alice Paul, and Carrie Chapman Catt. It filled me with pride to hear about such women of courage. When I went home and told my dad that someday I'd vote for a woman to be president, he hollered, "My daughters ain't never going to vote!"

Me and my big mouth shot back, "I will, too. So will Alice and Beulah. And Momma will vote in the next election." I should have kept my thoughts to myself.

The next week Miss Forester received a letter from some of the suffragists. They were working with Carrie Chapman Catt, the second most important woman in our country after Beulah's favorite movie star, Mary Pickford.

The suffragists wanted donations to buy a gift for Mrs. Catt, a sapphire and diamond brooch, to be presented at the victory celebration after enough states ratified.

On the walk home from school, my little sister Alice and I talked it over. I said I'd give a dime, and she decided to give a penny. After supper, we waited until Dad was out of earshot and asked Momma for the money.

"We need it to buy jewels for Charlie Chaplin's cat," Alice said.

I giggled as I set it all straight. Alice's face turned red when she found out she had mixed up Carrie Chapman Catt, the suffragist, with Charlie Chaplin, the funniest man in the movies.

Momma grinned, gave Alice a big old hug, and said we could have the money.

Right then, Dad walked in. "Have the money for what?" he bellowed.

Nobody answered, so he repeated hisself, I mean *himself*, and then turned on me. "Clara Fern, answer me *now!*"

I figured if I told a lie, I'd get a whipping. So I told the truth, and I got one anyhow.

You'd think I'd be used to Dad's angry nature. But the older I got, the more I thought somebody ought to stand up to him. And that's exactly what I did the day I turned fourteen.

That night at supper, the whole Massie family—me, Beulah, Alice, Bobby Earl, Momma, and my ornery dad—hunkered over the table eating sausage, fried eggs, and pinched-up biscuit covered with milk gravy. Because it was my birthday, October 21, 1919, Momma also cooked apples sprinkled with cinnamon. The smell of cinnamon tempted me to dream of far-off places: Madagascar, Ceylon, France, the Grand Canyon—places that Miss Forester showed us on the maps in our geography books. I hoped to see them someday if . . .

"Hot biscuits, Wilma!" Dad's booming order yanked me back to our farm kitchen. "And while you're at it, pour us some more blue john."

Momma brought him two steaming biscuits from the second batch out of the wood cookstove. She sat down again with a weary sigh. The lines creasing her thin face had deepened since morning. Dad had kept me home from school again, and all day Momma and I canned apple butter. I'm good and stout and can tolerate hard work. But Momma's puny, has been ever since she took sick with the influenza back in the winter.

She started pouring more skim milk into everybody's glass. When she got to mine, my mouth was full of apples, so I put my hand over the top. I swallowed. "I don't want *any* more." I said it nice, like Miss Forester taught me.

Momma stopped with the milk pitcher in midair.

"You heard me, Wilma. Pour!" Dad barked.

"No, thank you," is all I said, but plain and simple, my words meant, *You don't scare me.*

Dad's gray eyes threatened like a dark Ozark sky right before it becomes a toad strangler. Across the table, he got to his feet.

I'd had enough. I stood up, too. That caused him to fidget. I'm tall for a girl. Five feet, nine inches in my sock feet. My dad is barely five-foot-five.

"I don't want *any* more," I told him. "The blue john tastes blinky and ruins the flavor of the cinnamon."

"'Ruins the flavor of the cinnamon,'" he mimicked me in a high, squeaky voice. "Gettin' above your raisin', ain't you, Clara Fern? That teacher's puttin' fancy ideas into your head. I thought I learned you not to listen to that furriner."

I should have known better than to correct my dad. But I did it anyhow. "Miss Forester ain't . . . I mean *isn't* a foreigner, Dad."

"She's from Sant Louis, ain't she?"

"*Saint* Louis, Dad. Saint! Not 'Sant.' And St. Louis is in Missoura, the same state as our farm."

"She's got citified ways, and she ain't folks. She's a furriner."

I opened my mouth to explain it again, but he'd closed his ears.

"Pour Clara some milk, Wilma," he ordered.

Momma poured my glass half full and pleaded, "Just drink that much, Clara."

I shook my head. She knew I didn't like blue john. After the cream was saucered off the top of the raw milk and sold or used to make butter, we drank the watery liquid that was left, even after it clabbered.

"I won't drink any more blinky blue john."

"That better not be more sassin' I'm hearing," Dad yelled.

I grabbed the edge of the table, planted my big feet—what Momma calls my good understanding—and leaned in his direction.

"I'm fourteen now, Dad, and you're not the boss of me!"

His eyelids opened wide. I was reminded of the toad frogs over by the pond that peep and skip across the lily pads when you poke a stick at them.

Alice started coughing. She was covering up a belly laugh. She sputtered and blew bubbles in her milk to get herself under control. She's only nine, but we're alike. Except Alice is pretty with a round face, turned-up nose, and blonde hair. It's soft and nice, not like mine, which is the color of sand.

Seeing Alice nearly caused me to grin until I heard Dad.

"I said fill up the glass, Wilma!"

Momma aimed the pitcher at my glass. As Momma started pouring, I moved my hand to cover the top again. But I missed, hit the glass, and tipped it over. Momma kept pouring. Watery milk pooled on Bobby Earl's plate and drowned his runny eggs. Bobby Earl's seven and a half. Everybody says he favors Dad with his gray eyes and black hair. He bawled like a crybaby.

Dad hollered, "Stop pouring, Wilma!"

By the time she did, milk had splashed into the sorghum molasses and spread out every which way. When it ran off the table, soaking the laces of my black shoes, I stepped back and shook my foot.

My sister Beulah reached out with a napkin in her good hand and sopped up the milk that drained to her side of the table. "Don't let it run in my lap!" she whined.

Beulah is two years older than me, but she acts babyish on account of her being afflicted in her girlhood.

"I didn't get to finish," Bobby Earl whimpered.

"Hand me a dry rag," Beulah begged. "It's runnin' in my lap." She dropped the wet napkin and tried to roll her wicker wheelchair away from the table. But she started one of her coughing fits.

Then Alice jumped up and pulled Beulah's wheelchair way back to the wall. With a dishrag she dabbed at the milk splatters all over our sister.

Then Dad started in on me. "Sit down!" he ordered.

And I did.

"This is all your fault, Clara Fern! You're no good for nothin'. You growed so fast you're clumsy."

I slumped in my chair with my chin lowered to my chest. Blue john dripped off the table past my knee and puddled around the chair leg.

"Look at me when I'm talking to you!"

I looked at him, all right—I *glared* at him. "Dad, I'm not going to jump 'cause you say to!"

He stood there, fuming and fussing and shaking his fist at me. Everything but cussing. That's one thing my dad never did, no matter how aggravated he got.

"I've an idy you need punishin'." Dad never went past the first reader. He talked like the Ozark hillfolks that never got any book learning. "I've an idy to whip you."

I stiffened, not daring to tell him the word was "idea" not "idy."

"Bobby Earl, fetch me the strap," Dad commanded.

My brother raced out the door. I sat.

Alice made like she was helping clean up. I noted how she poured the rest of her blue john into the slop bucket for the hogs, when Dad's back was turned. Then she took the persimmon hickory-nut pie out of the pie safe and cut it into sections. Alice was smarter at getting by than I'd been at her same age, maybe than I'd ever be.

Momma cleared the dishes off the table, lifted up the soppy table-cloth, and spread out our other one. It looked dingy even though I'd rubbed my knuckles raw scrubbing it on the washboard.

She set out a clean fork and plate at Dad's place. Then, bless her heart, she took my part against Dad. "They's better ways to punish children, Henry."

"'Spare the rod and spoil the child.' That's what my grandpappy learned me."

I bit my lip to stop from blurting out, "Your grandpappy was an ignorant old hillbilly that never learned any better."

Dad glanced at the clean plate, then at the kitchen door. "Bobby Earl's taking his own sweet time."

Momma tried again. "Why don't you just make her clean up this mess and send her to bed? Tomorrow, she'll stay home again, and I'll work her hard. Woman's work is never done. There's floors to be mopped, and the rest of the canning, and Beulah to take care of. . . ." Her voice trailed off in a tired whisper.

I didn't want to miss school again, but I kept quiet.

"She'll clean it up," Dad yelled. "What's keeping that boy?"

He stomped over to the kitchen door, opened it, and peered out. Night was beginning to fall, and a chill wind blew yellow leaves into the room.

"Where's that strap, Bobby Earl?"

My brother stepped inside. "I couldn't find it, Dad." He stared at the floor.

"You better not be lyin' to me, boy!"

"I ain't, Dad. Honest." He crossed his heart.

"Who's been messin' with my strap?" Dad demanded.

I knew it wasn't Bobby Earl. Beulah couldn't have done it. She wouldn't have, anyway. She hadn't been whipped since the day before she fell out of the loft. I looked at Alice about the same time Dad did.

She was standing by our big sister, polite as can be, asking, "Do you care for a slice of pie, Sis?"

Beulah nodded sourly, her brown curls bouncing. She'd have been a pretty girl once. But with the pinched expression brought on by the pain in her spine, she looked downright mean.

Alice rolled the wheelchair back to the cleaned-up table. I glanced at Dad to see if his suspicions were as strong as mine. But he didn't seem to notice Alice's manners being any more refined than usual.

"Cut me a big slice while you're at it," Dad told her.

I figured his interest in persimmon hickory-nut pie was about to save my hide. I stood up.

"Where do you think you're going?" he demanded.

"To bed like Momma said."

"Not 'til I say, you ain't. Let's go." He headed toward the door.

"Can't it wait 'til morning?" Momma asked, her voice soft.

Dad was already out the door, commanding me to come on.

I hung back, praying for an angel of the Lord to fly down out of heaven and carry me to some far-off land.

Beulah chewed her pie, coughing between bites. Alice shrugged. If she was thinking I shouldn't have provoked Dad, I was of a mind to agree.

"I said to come on, Clara!" Dad screeched from the stoop.

I could barely see him in the dark.

"Better do like he says," Momma said.

After she said that, I knew any rescuing had to be by my own hand. I went to the kitchen door. Taller by four inches, I looked down into his stony eyes. "You aren't going to whip me, Dad!"

I took off running toward the dark Missoura woods behind the barn.

2

Treed Like a Critter

Running past the pond, I heard the toad frogs singing. In the twilight I could barely see. I slipped in cow-clods in the pasture. My stomach cramped, and I was breathing hard when I stopped at the tall maple by the sinkhole. But I didn't hear anybody following me. I clung to that old tree, taking in deep draughts of the chilly air. A slight wind rustled the leaves. The hoot of an owl echoed eerily through the timber.

The air was cold on my clammy skin. I was wearing a gingham frock, a hand-me-down. My leather shoes were stinking from the sour blue john mixed with cow filth. I wiped my soles on the leaves. A little filth wouldn't hurt me. Not as bad as a whipping. I looked up at the tree, wondering if I was too old to climb it and sit up there all night. Just then a whip-poor-will started its loud nightly call. *Whip-poor-will, poor-will, poor-will.* I'd climbed that maple a hundred times when I was little, but now I was too heavy for its old branches. The piercing scream of a mountain lion off in the timber caused me to settle on a plan. I'd spend the night in the barn. And in the morning, about dawn, before Dad went to do the milking, I'd sneak out and go on to school.

It wasn't easy finding my way across the pasture to the barn. But the light in the house kept me headed right. I took it slow. I nearly walked into the smokehouse, it was so pitch black. But the chicken coop was easy enough to miss because of the stench and the flutter of wings. At the barn, I ran my hand along the splintery wall boards until I found the latch and opened the creaky door. Inside, it was black like a cave. I stumbled over and climbed the rungs of the rickety ladder into the loft. I crawled across the warm, dry hay and lay down. Then I felt a tickle in my throat and my eyes watered. Hay dust. I sneezed. Once.

Twice. And wiped my nose on my sleeve. I heard a noise, this one more dangerous than the rats that were scratching in the corncrib.

My dad shouted out as he crossed the yard. "Clara, if you're still out in the timber, get on back here! You make me wait 'til morning and you'll get a whipping that will set you on fire."

I sat up, tense, pulled my knees up to my chin, and tucked my skirt under me. Through the loft opening, I saw the light of the lamp when he came into the barn.

"Clara Fern! If you're in this barn, face up to your punishment."

I felt another sneeze coming on. I pinched my earlobe hard and held my breath. The sneeze went away.

"Clara Fern! I'm warning you!"

I stayed as still as I could. But a tickle began in the back of my throat, and I sneezed.

Dad hee-hawed. "I knew you was up there!"

Next I heard Dad rattling the ladder. The floorboards of the loft quivered.

"You'll stay up there all night," he announced. "I pulled the ladder away. I'll be back in the morning." Carrying the lamp, he went back to the house, and I was treed like a critter.

Off and on during the night, I dozed. Twice, I heard the whistle of the train over by Winona. Then along about dawn, the barking of hounds chasing through the woods woke me. The shouts of hunters meant their hounds had treed a coon. I listened while the hunters felled the tree with axes to capture it.

I crawled over to the edge of the loft and looked at the ladder on the ground. It was a long way down. I walked the length of the loft and considered shinnying down one of the posts. If I worked up enough courage to try that and fell, like Beulah had done years before, there would be two of us rolling about in wicker wheelchairs.

Maybe I could drop onto something soft. I went to one of the openings in the loft floor. Grabbing the pitchfork out of a hay bale, I tossed loose hay down into the feed trough. When it was stacked high, I bent down on my knees, turned around, and scooted back until my long legs dangled over the opening. Holding onto the loft floor and a rough post that held up the roof, I stared down at that pile of hay and inched my way backward.

I closed my eyes and prayed. Right then, the barn door creaked open. I felt myself slipping, and I grabbed tight onto the edge of the loft. Splinters pierced my palms.

"Clara? If Dad sees you doing that, he'll really lay into you."

"Alice!" I clawed my way back up. "Don't just stand there. Hand up the ladder."

I brushed off the hay that clung to my rumpled frock.

"Dad's coming after he eats breakfast," she said.

"Then hurry!" I could barely keep from screaming.

"If he catches me, I'll get whipped, too."

"I'll run off before he gets here."

She shook her head. "There ain't time."

I wished she was close enough to shake. "Alice, please!"

"Last night, he found the strap where I hid it. If I help you, he'll know I done it."

"I'll give you my sock money," I told her. "It's underneath the mattress on my side of our bed."

"There's not enough in it."

Any other time, I'd demand to know when she found it. But Dad might be crossing the yard at that moment.

"You can have everything I own. 'Cause when I get away, I'm not coming back."

"I can have everything?" Alice liked finery. She wanted the crocheted doilies and delicate shawl Momma kept for me in a trunk.

Not wanting to give up my prettiest things, I hesitated, but only for a second. "You can even have the heirloom lace Aunt Daisy left me."

"You can't get away. Where would you go?"

To school, I almost said. But if Dad thought Miss Forester had taken me in, he'd never let Alice go to school again.

"Granny 'hite's."

"Dad will fetch you back."

Granny 'hite lived down in the hollow, way back in the jillikens in Casto Valley. But it was close enough for Dad to find me.

"Then I'll go to the city. Like Opal did."

Opal Wilhite was our older cousin, who had a job in Kansas City. She was a Harvey Girl and made good wages serving meals to passengers waiting for trains.

"Opal's visiting Granny right now. At Sunday school last week, she told me about her job. She'll be going back to work soon, and I'll go with her."

"Do you mean it?"

"Yes, that's what I'll do," I said, hoping to convince myself that it was possible. "And I'll get a job and send you money."

Alice cackled. "Doing what? You ain't old enough to get a good job."

"Even if I have to work in a toothpaste factory filling up tubes, I'll get a job."

At school, we'd seen a picture in a *National Geographic* of girls working in a factory. They sat on wooden chairs in front of big containers full of toothpaste. A man—Miss Forester thought he was their manager—stood behind them. Underneath the picture it said that each girl could fill ten thousand tubes a day.

"You can have all my things here, Alice, and I'll send you some of my wages."

I wanted to ask her to peek out the barn door to see if Dad was on his way, but if I spooked her, she'd protect her own hide, not mine. My underarms felt moist and my heart thumped almost loud enough to hear.

"I don't know. . . ."

"Alice, if I get caught, I'll swear you had nothing to do with me getting out of the loft, and you can still have the sock money."

"And Aunt Daisy's lace?"

"Yes!"

She took her slow time doing it, but finally she propped the ladder up against the loft and steadied it while I climbed down. Any second, Dad could open that creaky door. I laid the ladder back on the ground so he wouldn't be sure how I escaped.

I rushed to the end stall to get out of the barn on the side away from the house.

Alice was right behind me. "Send me a postal card. And one to Miss Forester. She'll be sad that you quit school." Outside, she tugged at my frock and stopped. "Don't forget me."

I kept going another step, then turned back because of the tears in her voice. I bent down to hug her, and she threw her arms up around my neck.

I heard Dad shout from inside the barn. "Clara, come on down!"

I pulled away. Across the pasture and into the timber, I ran toward Granny 'hite's.

3

No Place Else to Run

I ran through the woods, stumbling over dead logs and rocks covered by fallen leaves. I twisted my ankle when I scrambled off a small hill sideways. Pain streaked up my leg, adding to the misery of splinters in my palms. My leather shoes were blistering my heels. Well out of sight of the farmhouse, I finally slowed up. It was too far to run the whole way to Granny 'hite's.

Cardinals whistled *what-cheer-cheer-cheer* and flitted through the timber. Squirrels scampered up tree trunks. The leaves were ablaze in autumn's colors. The sky was the deep blue of Indian summer.

Picturing Dad coming after me, I kept hiking toward the old Wilhite homestead. It lay three miles west of our farm among the dogwood and black walnut trees of Casto Valley. Dad wouldn't chase me through the timber. He'd hitch up Old Dan to the wagon. That would take him some time because of the heavy harness. Then he'd take the long, winding road. When I got to Granny's, would he be standing on her porch? Scary as that thought was, I had no place else to go.

More thirsty than hungry, I found a spring, bent down, cupped the bubbling water with my hands, and drank. Through the trees, I heard the rumble of a wagon on the road. The rapid clomping of horses' hooves told me the driver was in a hurry. I jumped to my tortured feet and took off running again.

When I came to the dry creek bed that bordered Granny's property, I ran down the middle of it. There was no underbrush to tangle around my feet, but the big chunks of chert tried to pierce the soles of my shoes. Osage Indians used these rocks to make sharp points for their spears. Old-timers have picked up ancient arrowheads from their plowed fields.

When I reached the dark cave at the bottom of the bluff, I considered crawling into it. I didn't stop, though. Not 'til I got to Granny's. Then I leaned against a cottonwood to catch my breath. My ankle was swelling, and my heels were stuck to the shoe leather where the blisters had burst. After a bit, I sneaked up to the back of Granny's log cabin.

I peered around the trunk of a black walnut. On the hill sat the chicken coop. I could see past the privy and up the hollow into the cornfield full of fodder teepees. The milk cow ambled through a section of fence where the rails had rotted. She mooed and flicked her stub of a tail at the flies buzzing around her. Two crows flew off a rusted plow half-hidden in a clump of dried chigger weed. I strained to see if a wagon was coming down the dirt road.

"Who's sneaking around my place?" demanded an ancient voice.

I whirled around to face Granny 'hite, a tiny, bat-faced woman.

"Cat got your tongue, gal?" Her voice was raspy. Her knobby finger pointed at me the way it had when I was little.

"It's Clara Massie, Granny." My voice wobbled and scratched, and I cleared my throat to cover up for sounding addled.

"Massie?" She gripped her burlap sack and studied my face.

"Clara. Henry's second daughter."

"Ida's granddaughter?" Ida was Granny 'hite's sister, my dad's mother and my grandmother. Granny 'hite wasn't really my granny.

"Yes, Granny. I'm Clara." I shifted my weight from one burning, blistered foot to the other.

"You favor my sister Ida. You have her freckles and light hair. And she was right tall, too."

"You told me that the last time I visited." Dad claimed Granny was tetched because of her forgetfulness.

"Somebody took sick on your place? Somebody needin' Granny's doctorin'?"

"Nobody's sick. I came to see Opal."

She squinted at me.

"Your granddaughter. Is Opal still here?"

"How's that afflicted sister of yourn?" Granny asked.

"Beulah's managing." I glanced toward the cabin. Of course, Opal was still there. She had to be. "Beulah has a bad cough the doctor's treating, but . . ."

"If it's the grippe, the town doctor can't cure her."

My momma said Granny was the best of the old granny women in our neck of the woods. She had an Indian doctor book and doctored folks for free with sassafras tea to thin the blood or her famous black draught, a mix of turpentine, kerosene, and skunk grease. It makes a powerful poultice and an all-around good remedy if it doesn't burn the hide off while it's working.

"I told Henry he should've called Granny 'hite when Beulah was afflicted," she went on. "I might'a cured that gal, but tuberculosis of the spine set in 'fore I could help." Granny called every serious ailment tuberculosis.

"Did your ma send you for black walnuts?" she demanded, rattling her burlap sack.

"No, Granny. I came to talk to Opal."

"Then you best hurry. She was fixin' to leave when I left the cabin."

My throat constricted.

Granny walked toward the cabin, indicating with a wave of her gnarled hand that I was to follow. The only thing that kept me from charging around her was the awful pain in my feet and ankle.

We had reached the porch when the front door opened. My pretty, dark-haired, citified cousin Opal stepped out, carrying a leather valise. Slouching like a debutante, she was dressed for traveling in a chemise day frock made of gray jersey cloth. It came just below her knees. Her stockings were soft gray, and her pumps were polished black.

Tears of joy flooded my eyes. "Opal, thank goodness."

"Clara, what a surprise!" A pleasant laugh bubbled out of her. She set her valise down and reached out to hug me. I bested her height by five inches, but worse than that, I was filthy. There was no telling how much hay still clung to my hair. I brushed away two ticks crawling on my frock. It was no use picking at the beggar lice that stuck to my skirt.

Opal looked me up and down, but she was polite.

Granny didn't hold back, though. "Don't she look like a bobcat that's been drug tailfirst through the briar patch?"

I backed away. "I ran all the way through the woods."

Opal patted my shoulder. "Shouldn't you be in school? Do your folks know you're here?"

"Well, not exactly. . . . I'm ready to go to the city and get a job."

Granny frowned, but it was Opal that laid into me.

"At Sunday school, I told you to finish school. When you're eighteen, come to Kansas City, and then I'll put in a good word for you."

"But I'm ready to go now. You said I'd make a good Harvey Girl."

Right then, Granny dropped her sack. It thudded on the wooden floor beside Opal's valise. "Company's coming," she announced, pointing down the road

I noticed a swirl of dust behind a blackberry thicket in the distance.

"Oh no!" I groaned.

I took off running into the woods. At first, I was only aware of my swollen ankle and tender feet. I could barely stand the pain. But I hadn't gone far when I heard *Oogah, oogah* and the chugging of a Tin Lizzie on Granny's road. *Oogah, oogah.*

I turned back, taking careful steps. I stepped onto the porch as the flivver slowed up to straddle two chuckholes in the rutted road. Its fenders flapped the last few yards, and it hissed when it stopped. The top was down, and the driver waved. Clad in ritzy motoring togs, a duck-billed cap, and goggles, he squeezed the bulb horn once more. *Oogah.* When he slipped his goggles up on his forehead, I saw it was Duey Bandy.

"Howdy, Clara," Duey said after he spoke to Opal and Granny. "Do you remember me?"

"Sure," I told him. "I haven't seen you in a month of Sundays, not since . . ." I stopped, remembering the last time was at the memorial service for his brother, who died in the war. "Are you living around here again?"

"Just visiting—family and old friends," he said, glancing at Opal in an admiring way. "And offering a friend a ride down to the depot to catch a train."

Opal laughed her bubbly laugh and picked up her valise.

"I'll get that," Duey said, jumping out from behind the wheel. He set her nice valise in the backseat and opened the passenger door. Elegantly, she stepped onto the running board. Then she sat down on the leather seat and smoothed out her skirt.

I wanted to beg her not to leave. But the words jammed up on my tongue.

"Ought to come in an' set a spell," Granny said.

I could have hugged her neck.

"Duey, would you care to come in the cabin?" Opal asked.

I added, "Yes, come in and visit."

"Thank you," he said to Opal, "but if we're going to make it to the depot in time to catch your train, we'd better be on our way."

Opal didn't protest.

Duey slipped his goggles back down over his eyes and started up the motorcar. He nodded to me and Granny.

"Opal, take me with you," I pleaded.

Opal raised an eyebrow.

"Please." I stepped toward the flivver. There was plenty of room for a passenger in the backseat. "I have to go to Kansas City."

"Today?" she asked over the rattling of the engine. With the look she gave me, she might as well have added, *Dressed like that?*

"I can clean up at the depot."

"Clara, what about school? What about your family?"

I stared at my hurting feet and lowered my voice. "Opal, I can't go back home. I have to get a job."

Duey interrupted impatiently. "We need to be on our way."

Opal said, "If you had told me sooner, Clara, we might have worked something out." She looked glum, but then her face brightened. "I'll send you a railroad pass so you can come and visit me."

"Send it to me here at Granny's," I yelled while they pulled away.

I watched the dust tail swirl behind the automobile until they were out of sight. Then I slumped down onto Granny's creaking wooden steps and hung my head.

Granny picked up her sack of black walnuts and went into the cabin. I sat there and cried for a while. Then I untied my shoelaces and pulled off my shoes. The skin on my heels ripped away, leaving fiery patches of oozing flesh. Even worse was my inflamed ankle. It looked twice its normal size.

I looked up to see Granny bending over me. She held a tin of skunk grease to treat my sores. But she was staring down the road. She had a peculiar expression on her wrinkled face. "More company's comin'."

I didn't hear or see anything.

"Best run and hide, gal. It's your dad coming to fetch you."

I didn't stop to prove whether she was right. I'd hide in the cave under the bluff. I got to my bare feet and took two steps before I cried out. I could barely walk.

"Into the cabin with you, gal," Granny ordered. "Take them shoes and get inside, I tell you."

In agonizing pain, I hobbled into the front room. It took a second for my eyes to adjust to the darkness. Where would I hide? Behind the settee? In Granny's bedroom? Or up the stairs? The sight of the narrow, wooden stairs threw a scare into me.

I remembered a time when I was little and I'd been playing on those stairs. Granny had shouted at me, "Raw Head and Bloody Bones is up there! Raw Head and Bloody Bones'll get little kids who don't mind their elders!"

What was up those stairs? Nothing so scary, I assured myself, as my dad bearing down Granny's road. I was fourteen now—too old and too tall to be scared. I forced myself to climb the stairs, step by tortuous step. It was so dark on the second story, I could barely see. I took another step and tripped over a small valise. I landed on my knees as the shoes I'd been carrying thudded onto the floor. I lay down and cried.

Within a couple of minutes I heard a wagon pull up outside. I could hear voices. Then heavy footsteps stomped into the cabin.

"Where is she, Granny?" my dad demanded.

"You took your own sweet time gettin' here, Henry," Granny chided him.

"I ain't got time to do your chores, Granny. Got my own to do," my dad shouted. "Get away from them stairs."

"You're my only kinfolk still around these parts," she said. "It falls to you to help an old granny woman."

"My farm comes first. Stand aside. Is Clara up them stairs?"

I stopped breathing.

"There's work to be done up there, too, Henry. I need that chest o' drawers hauled down. You go on up and carry that chest down here for Granny."

By then, my eyes had adjusted to the dark. There was no chest in the room. Granny was bluffing.

"I ain't horsing no old chest down them stairs, Granny." Footsteps stomped back across the room, and my dad's voice came from farther off. "Granny, you tell Clara I'll track her down."

My body shook with relieved sobs when I heard his wagon pull away.

4

A Ticket to Travel

Thunder rumbled and clapped, and jagged streaks of lightning flashed across the coal-dark afternoon sky. Raindrops pelted my head and stung my cheeks and hands. I ran for Granny 'hite's cabin.

I had been out walking, up to the boundary of Granny's farm where her road intersects with the one that heads down to Winona and the train depot. I had smoothed on Granny's remedy, bandaged my ankle and feet, eased them into my shoes, and trekked down to the crossroads, hoping that Duey and Opal would come back. But they'd been gone a whole day.

I knew they wouldn't come back for me, but I discovered that Opal had left her train case. It was the valise I'd tripped over hiding from Dad. It matched the one Duey had set in the backseat. I figured she left it by mistake when I surprised her on the porch.

Drenched, I reached the edge of the porch. Rain pounded into the ground. Spots of mud bounced up onto my black shoes. Mud dribbled down my wet dress from my knees to the hem at my ankles. I stepped back against the log wall, pulled my braid around beneath my chin, and wrung the water out.

I considered walking the twelve miles down to the depot, right then, with the storm rampaging around me. But if I made it all the way to the depot, what would I do? Train tickets cost money. Where was I going to get money?

The good thing was Dad hadn't come back yet. Partly because of the hard rain, I figured. The mudholes blocking the road would most likely keep him home another few days. The thought that kept me going from hour to hour was that Opal promised she'd send me a railroad pass.

"Lord 'ave mercy, gal! There won't be no sunshine yet awhile." Granny had sneaked up on me again. I hadn't heard her because of the lightning crashes. "Come on in, and get into some dry clothes."

"I didn't bring any, Granny." My voice shook from trying to talk through chattering teeth.

"I've some old things you can make do," she said in her raspy voice.

I doubted she had anything big enough to fit me, but I followed her.

The cabin was warm and dry. The heat from the wood cookstove and the smell of cornbread hot out of the oven soothed me. The kitchen table was set with two chipped white plates, two bent forks, and two canning jars for glasses.

"Take off them wet clothes," Granny directed me.

She went into another room while I struggled to untie the wet laces of my shoes and slip out of them. Then I peeled the clinging cotton off my skin. Granny was back by the time my soiled frock lay on top of my shoes in a muddy pile. I stayed in my underthings even though they were soaked, too. If I sat near enough to the stove while we ate, they'd dry with me inside them. The quilt she handed me was a log cabin pattern, the same as the one Alice and I slept under.

Granny noticed me inspecting it. "Ida, your grandma, pieced it."

At the sink, I pumped water into a bowl and grated a pile of soap chips off the cake of lye soap. I lathered my hands all the way up to my elbows, rinsed the harsh soap off as best I could in the cold water, and dried with a flour sack. Then I wrapped the soft quilt around me and sat down at the table. Granny placed my shoes closer to the stove, picked up my frock, and carried it dripping out on the porch.

We ate cornbread, canned green beans and sliced potatoes boiled in salt pork, spiced peaches, and wild blackberry jam. We drank fresh milk with the cream rising to the top. It was a fine meal—except when Granny set the butter out. There were grease ants crawling in it, which I scraped off.

That's when I realized how poor her eyesight was. I pitied her living all alone with nobody to help her. Except when Opal came twice a year. My dad ought to be horsewhipped for not coming on the place no more often than he did. Maybe that explained why he hadn't come back after me—he'd be obliged to help with Granny's chores.

After we wiped the dishes, she lit a coal-oil lamp and led me through the cabin. She had something to show me. We passed by the narrow stairs leading to the upper story where I'd slept the last two nights. I recalled again how I'd misbehaved when I was little. And Granny had warned me not to play on the steps.

"Raw Head and Bloody Bones isn't living up there anymore," I said.

Granny gave me a squinty-eyed look. Then I grinned.

"Tellin' that story was the best way to keep you young'uns from gettin' hurt. Them stairs is dangerous. I fell down 'em when I was carrying my youngest, Irene, and she was born afflicted."

That's the first time anyone ever told me of a reason for Irene's affliction. She grew to be a woman with the mind and voice of a child, always hugging her baby doll close to her heart and singing it a lullaby. She was tenderhearted and acted sweet to everybody. About the only thing she ever learned how to do was make buttonholes. And folks bragged on her ability to play the piano in church. She played by ear. When Irene died at the age of forty, Granny buried her in a wooden coffin with her baby doll beside her.

With the flickering lamplight throwing her shadow against the wall, Granny led me on into her bedroom. She took a tiny key out of her chest of drawers.

"Ought to be some clothes in there you could make do."

She crooked her finger at an old wooden trunk in the corner of the room. She held the lamp above me as I knelt and unlocked each of the two locks.

"Ain't been open in more'n twenty years, I 'spect."

I lifted the lid. The trunk could have been packed the week before by the looks of the clothes. Except that they were wrinkled and out of fashion. There were lacy, beribboned drawers and underpetticoats, and long, lovely dresses, all handstitched but as nice as any ready-to-wear clothes.

"Who sewed these?" I pulled out a silk dress with embroidered trim on the bodice and a navy wool traveling suit with black braid trim.

"Ida. She was a fine seamstress."

After I'd laid out a few dresses across the bed, I held the prettiest up against my tall body.

"Slip it on," she said. "Looks like it'll fit."

I wanted nothing more than to put on that dress. It had yards and yards of green flowered cotton in the bodice and flowing skirt. The long sleeves were fitted to the lacey wrists and puffed under ruffles at the shoulders. The center of the bodice front was a gathered sheer fabric—batiste, Granny told me—with two rows of ruffles and a trim of pink flowers. The high collar and the sash around the waist were white satin.

"Ought to try it, gal. Ida would want you to."

Granny 'hite set the lamp on the chest of drawers and handed me some of the underthings to change into first. I wriggled out of my damp ones, then slipped on the dress. She helped me fasten the long row of buttons up the back and tie the big satin bow. It fit me perfectly.

Granny dug through the trunk and handed up a bouquet of pink flowers that matched the trim on the bodice. Then she gave me a short veil of lace, satin, and more pink flowers.

She stood up, squinted, and admired the dress—and me. "Hit was Ida's wedding dress," she said at a higher-than-usual pitch, "and wearin' it, you could pass for her twin, I do declare."

I saw the tear Granny wiped from the corner of her eye.

After a little while, I took the dress off, refolded it, and repacked the trunk, keeping out some of the underthings and a sensible frock.

Before we headed off to bed, we set a spell in the kitchen. I let down my braid to finish drying my hair.

"You look like you need cheerin', gal," Granny said when I'd been quiet too long. "I've a picture that'll bring a smile to that long face."

She left the kitchen, and I could hear her rummaging around in the other room. Pretty soon, she came back with a small basket. She opened the lid and dumped the contents on the table. There were postal cards and photographs and dollar bills.

"Them things are what Opal sent me from out West," Granny explained. "Here," Granny said after she separated the postal cards from the pictures. "Opal in her Harvey Girl uniform."

I looked at my cousin.

"Opal stayed with me a month this time. She cleaned up inside the cabin. It was right pleasant to have her about the place. And such a good worker, too. She would come more often 'cept she only gets a month off ever six months. The rest of the time she's waitressin'. Says it's hard work, but excitin'. Pay's good."

In the picture, Opal had her brown hair parted in the middle, smoothed away from her face, and pinned back. Her Harvey Girl uniform was a long black dress with a white pinafore over it. Under her white collar was a black bow tie, and her shoes and stockings were black. She looked crisp and starched.

Some folks, including my dad, insisted she should get married, then do for her husband and children. That it wasn't a girl's place to leave home and go off to the city to work, especially as a waitress. That nothing good would ever come of it. But the smile on Opal's face made me think Dad wasn't telling the whole story. And I vowed to do the same as her as soon as I had the chance.

The stack of postal cards fascinated me. Opal had sent them from California, New Mexico, Texas, Arizona.

"Are your feet itchy like Opal's?" Granny asked when she saw me studying the cards.

"You mean my blisters? They'll heal quick enough thanks to your remedy." I looked over to see her grinning.

"Now that I think on it, Ida's were right itchy, too. Folks say there's only one cure if you're born with itchy feet."

"What's that?"

"Travel."

"I never had a name for my affliction until now, but I guess I do have itchy feet. I'm longing to visit some exciting places." I flipped through two more cards. "My Grandma Massie had itchy feet? Nobody ever told me that."

"It's just like your dad not to talk about her. Him and his branch of the family never approved of Ida's ramblings."

"Where did she go?"

"St. Louis."

I laid the cards aside and stared at Granny while she told the whole story.

"Ida was happy married to Marvin the whole time he was working at the sawmill over to West Eminence. Then he took a dangerous job as a brakeman on the railroad. Not more than six months later, he was killed in an accident. Left her all alone with a young'un to raise."

"My dad?"

Granny nodded. "Might have been around 1895, as I recollect. Your dad would've been eight years old. But I disremember the exact date. She was twenty-five. She figured if she went to the city she could work as a seamstress, sewing fine clothes for rich folks."

"What did she do with my dad?"

"Marvin's folks took him in. Ida worked hard and sent most of her wages home for Henry's raisin'. Ida came home one time, thinking she'd take Henry back with her. But by then, he'd been told all manner of hurtful things about her. He must have been ten or twelve at the time. And he'd have nothin' to do with her. She begged and pleaded, but he couldn't be convinced. So she went back without him. She kept on sending him money, though. Right up until she died."

We were quiet for a while. I read the rest of the postal cards. "If I only visit one far-away place, here's the one I want to see." I held out a picture of the Grand Canyon.

Granny tapped it with her finger. "I'm partial to that one myself."

"It explains on the back that this is a lithograph of a painting by Thomas Moran."

I'd once seen a photo of the well-known painter himself, sitting on the rim of the canyon with his two daughters. They peered over his shoulder as he painted the majestic canyon scene—the raging Colorado River cutting through the middle of rugged mountains tinted purple, cream, and rust.

I read Granny what it said on the back of the card. "Teddy Roosevelt claimed the Grand Canyon is the one great sight that every American should see."

My eyes wandered from the card to the dollar bills lying next to Opal's photograph on the table.

As if she knew what I was thinking, Granny said, "You take that money, gal. Buy yourself a cure for itchy feet."

"Cure?"

She tilted her head and grinned. "A ticket to travel."

5

Out of the Ozarks

"We wasn't expectin' to see any of you'uns this time of year," said Rachel Hines from the passenger's side of her freight wagon. She was a cousin on my momma's side of the family.

Her husband was driving their team of mules down to the train depot to pick up goods they'd ordered from the Sears and Roebuck catalogue. Accepting her offer of a ride, I bounced along in the back of the big wagon with one arm resting on Opal's leather train case. Granny 'hite's straw valise packed with a few of Grandma Massie's old clothes lay on the other side.

I had on Grandma Massie's navy wool traveling suit with its full skirt that reached my ankles, one of which was still bandaged. It fit fine. But I worried that I looked old-fashioned, like a picture I'd seen in an old Butterick magazine my momma kept in the attic. Rachel's disapproving look confirmed it. I gazed at the red barn we were passing, hoping my cheeks weren't that same color.

As I was jostled along on a washboard part of the road, I stared out across the Ozark hills where all the trees had been cut down. Clear cutting, it's called. For years, men had felled nearly every good stand of timber around and operated sawmills, cutting hundreds of board feet a day. Only a few acres remained where the owners refused to sell their trees. Most places, there was nothing left but rocky hills with soil too poor to grow crops on. Then brambles intertwined with poison ivy would take over. The desire to leave that wasted Missoura land behind and set out on a grand adventure bucked up my spirit.

When we finally got to Winona, it was almost dark. Rachel's husband slowed the mules right in front of the train depot, and I grabbed Opal's train case and Granny's straw valise and jumped down off the wagon.

As she waved goodbye, Rachel's expression showed she had some misgivings about leaving me there after dark. Until they pulled away, I smiled confidently, even though underneath the surface I was jittery. Then I walked over to the depot.

The only light was in the telegraph office. When I pecked on the window, the night dispatcher ignored me. He didn't come to the door until he finished tapping out two night letters.

"Sorry, Miss, but we're closed," he told me. He appeared to be not much older than me. Beneath his green eyeshade, his face was begrimed with smudges off the carbon paper he used to make copies. And he was friendly enough.

"Can I buy a ticket to Kansas City?"

"The ticket office opens at eight a.m."

Behind him, another message started coming in. He shut the door and returned to his telegraph key.

All night I sat on a wooden bench right outside the ticket office window. The sound of the ticker was my only company. Unless you count the noise of the two freight trains that roared down the tracks. It got cold that night. I huddled in the knitted shawl I pulled out of my valise. In the morning, I tried the door of the ladies' restroom, but it was locked. Then I paced around the platform next to the tracks until I warmed up. When the ticket office opened at one minute after eight, I was the first in line.

"May I help you?" the bald man behind the counter asked.

"I hope so, " I began. "I need to get this train case to my cousin Opal Wilhite. She's a Harvey Girl in Kansas City."

He glanced at the people already behind me. "The freight window is right over there."

"I want to take it to her." I set the train case down and laid the dollars Granny loaned me on the counter.

"Miss, that will buy you a ticket to Springfield."

"But I have to get to Kansas City."

"You'll either need more money or a pass."

"A pass?" I asked.

"People who work for the railroad have passes," he said. "All Fred Harvey employees are issued passes. Like your cousin. You said she was a Harvey Girl. She'd have a . . . " He scratched his bald head. "Wait a minute. I remember her. About the middle of last week. She said she'd left her pass somewhere. She tried to sweet talk me into letting her ride for free. How could I be sure if she was a Harvey Girl?"

"What did she do?"

"She borrowed money from the gentleman escorting her."

"What am I going to do? This is all the money I have."

"I can sell you a ticket to Springfield, Miss."

I bought it and walked away, trying not to worry about what I was going to do when I stepped off the train there. By then, I was desperate for the restroom. After setting my bags on the floor, I used the toilet. Then I washed my hands at a washbasin. I splashed some water on my face and checked the glass. I needed a hairbrush. Hoping there might be one in Opal's train case, I snapped open the latch. There were some underthings and a pair of blue silk pajamas folded on the top. They smelled nice, like the fancy cologne she'd let me smell one time. I reached down past them and felt around. I found a brush. And then tucked down to one side, I also found Opal's coin purse. Inside it were seven dollar bills, a five-dollar bill, a coin purse jammed full of dimes, and her Harvey Girl railway pass.

"The Horrible and Slow Jolting." That's what the men at the Farmer's Exchange call the train from Winona to Springfield. I climbed aboard full of hope. In the gangway I held my breath as I passed several spittoons. It didn't take long to find a seat next to a young woman holding a whimpering baby.

Despite the odor of soiled diapers, sour milk, and spittoons, the first few miles were a luxury after riding in the freight wagon. Traveling by train included the swaying bounce of the day coach, the metallic click, click, click of wheels along the steel rails, the toot of the whistle at crossings, and the flat farmland across the bottom of the Show Me State whizzing past the window.

The Springfield depot was bigger and more crowded than the one at Winona, but it wasn't much to brag on. I spent most of my time finding out which train I had to catch to get to Kansas City, then standing in a long line and showing the ticket agent Opal's Harvey Girl pass. He didn't blink an eye, just handed me a ticket to Union Station.

I borrowed a few dimes from Opal's coin purse, counting carefully so I'd know how much to pay her back. I bought a boxed supper from a news-butcher, hawking newspapers and cigars to the passengers next to the tracks. I sat down on a bench to eat. Inside the shoebox was a shriveled up piece of fried chicken, a boiled egg, a slice of stale light bread smeared with rancid butter, and a piece of apple pie. The egg smelled spoiled, the apples were sour as green persimmons, and the chicken was tough. But I was famished and ate every awful bite.

The day coach to Kansas City was cleaner and plusher than the one from Winona. There were no colicky babies, and a big sign on the mahogany paneling at the front prohibited spitting, although several men were puffing smelly cigars.

After I shoved my valise and the train case onto the metal rack overhead, I sat on a padded, velour seat next to a portly lady with a wide smile. Mrs. Wilder, she said her name was. She was telling about the trips she'd made when she interrupted herself, "Why, honey, you're looking pale. Do you feel okay?"

I didn't answer as I slipped out of Grandma Massie's wool jacket.

"Did you eat something that didn't agree with you? Railway food is notoriously bad."

I concentrated on the coach's domed ceiling.

"I recommend eating at a Harvey House. Their chefs know how to prepare gourmet meals. Oyster stew, breaded veal cutlets, chicken croquettes, mince pies."

The mention of food, even good food, made me gag like the time Doc Adams poked a splintery tongue depressor down my throat.

"One time, I was traveling through Kansas when we stopped for dinner at a Harvey eatery. . . . Say, are you all right?"

Gagging, I held my hands over my mouth.

"I know what you need." She dug around in her tapestry bag and pulled out a folded paper poke. "This is just the thing if you can't make it to the privy at the end of the car."

I took the bag and fanned my face.

"Fresh air might help," she suggested. "Open that window."

That sounded easy, but as I struggled to my feet, the train lurched and my knees buckled. After two tries, I managed to hang on to the seat in front of me and raise up the heavy window about four inches. The wind rushing into the stuffy coach reeked of coal smoke. Cinders sprinkled my white shirtwaist when I sat down.

"Well, as I was saying," my traveling companion continued, "train travel has improved, but I've heard stories about the bad food in the old days." She chuckled.

My skin felt clammy.

"Used to be that just before the train pulled into a station, the conductors collected a half dollar for each meal. They kept ten cents, and the rest went to the eatery owners. When the train stopped, the passengers rushed into the dining room. What was set before them on dirty linen was fatty bacon, heavy biscuits called sinkers, and coffee that was bitter as acorns. But worst of all was 'railroad pie.' Some diners claimed the crust tasted like sawdust, the gravy like glue, and the meat like prairie dog."

I wondered if I could make it down the swaying aisle to the privy.

"Then the passengers would begin to eat, but the engineer would toot his whistle and the conductor would yell 'Boaaarrrrd!' The passengers had to scramble back to the train, leaving most of the vittles."

"Please . . . stop." I whispered.

"And here's the part that will turn your stomach. The food left on the plates was scraped back into the pots and served to the next travelers."

My stomach did turn—inside out into the paper poke.

"You poor dear," she said, "you really were sick."

I folded down the top inch of the paper poke and laid it on the floor. I rested my head against the seat and closed my eyes. The rhythmic clicking of the wheels soothed me. I slept for quite a while.

When I woke, cramped and stiff, the lights were on in the day coach and it was dark outside.

"See the lights of the city up ahead?" the chatty lady asked. "We're almost to the Kansas City Union Station."

I leaned into the window, which someone had closed, and watched the twinkling lights. Passengers began moving about, gathering their belongings. As we slowed to a stop at the station, I read the names of other arriving and departing trains—Kansas Pacific, Union Pacific, Atchison, Topeka, Santa Fe, and dozens more.

A black porter carried luggage up to the vestibule. Standing in the gangway, he whisk-broomed some passengers' suits and felt hats before they disembarked. I declined his offer, thinking the service might cost money.

Off the train with my valise under one arm and Opal's train case under the other, I trudged in the direction the porter had pointed out. "The Harvey lunchroom?" he'd said. "Walk to the end of the waiting room. When you pass through the arch, make a left turn at the grand clock. You can't miss it."

Moving with the shuffling crowd in the long waiting room, I saw a ladies washroom sign. Inside, I rinsed out my mouth and brushed away some of the coal dust, then I ventured back into the crowd. I'd never seen hundreds of people in one place before, not even at the Old Settlers Reunion.

The grand clock in the arch was too big to miss, being about as wide as I am tall. In the Grand Hall there was a barbershop, a newsstand and bookstore, a candy store, a toy store, and a drugstore. All the shops were well lit and open, even though it was late at night. The ornate ceiling, which was about a hundred feet off the floor, was beautifully painted in what I overheard a woman call Wedgewood blue and dusty rose. The fancy names suited those fancy colors. The three chandeliers were another sight to see. That gigantic station must have cost thousands of dollars to build.

Finally, I spotted the sign for the Fred Harvey lunchroom. I'd missed it, even though the porter said I couldn't. I'd gawked so much that I walked in a circle twice. Inside the glass doors, I stopped. The aroma of fresh-baked pastries and roasted meats mingled in the huge gray and pink room. Citified men in fine black suits and chic ladies sat on high-backed swivel stools at an oblong lunch counter. It had a shiny, marble top. Behind it, Harvey Girls carried trays balanced on their palms, filled glasses with tinkling iced drinks, or set tempting dishes before customers. I felt out of place and about as stylish as Hayburn, our old Missoura mule that we kids dressed up one time in a straw hat. Had my dad been right about us Massies not fitting in with 'furriners'?

6

No More Blinky Milk

Several people crowded in behind me. "Excuse me, Miss," a man with a gruff voice said.

My straw valise and Opal's train case were still bundled under my arms.

"Please let us pass."

I turned to see a tightly corseted woman in a hat trailing ostrich plumes.

"Our train leaves in twenty minutes," she said.

A gray-haired man approached. "Welcome to Fred Harvey's. Would you care to eat in the dining room or at our lunch counter?"

I answered honestly. "I'm looking for my cousin."

He cast a disapproving eye over my wrinkled traveling suit. "There's an empty seat on this side of the counter, Miss. Follow me."

I did, thinking his preacher suit and citified manners meant he was the boss. He led me to the far side of the long marble counter and held the swivel seat while I tried to sit in it. But I couldn't with those grips under my arms.

"Let me set your bags on the floor, Miss." He placed them next to my feet. "Now try it."

I sat.

"Enjoy your meal."

"Excuse me, sir," I said, "do you know where I might find my cousin Opal Wilhite?"

"Not off hand, Miss." He walked away, smirking.

Every seat on either side of me along the counter was taken. More customers occupied the seats on the opposite side. Inside the counter, eight or ten Harvey Girls were hard at work, but none of them was Opal.

The girls bustled back and forth serving customers seated at the counter or at tables against the walls. They filed in and out of the swinging doors to the kitchen with trays balanced above one shoulder. Customers constantly gave them orders. Several girls spent their whole time filling cups with steaming coffee from the spigots of huge, chrome-plated coffee urns. The urns were sitting on beautiful mahogany and glass pastry cases. One peek at the desserts in those glass cases tempted my mouth to water. There were doughnuts dusted with sugar, layer cakes, piles of oatmeal cookies, and wedges of fruit and cream pies.

"What would you like to drink, Miss?" one of the Harvey Girls asked me.

"Oh, I . . . uh . . . I'm looking for my cousin."

She smiled pleasantly. "I'd be happy to bring you something to drink while you wait. We have milk, hot tea, iced tea, or our famous coffee. It's fresh-brewed and always delicious. I recommend it. If you're a coffee drinker."

Could she tell how young I was?

"How about a cup of Ovaltine?"

"Ovaltine?" I repeated. I stiffened my back, trying to look eighteen.

"Coffee, please," I said, looking her straight in the eye and daring her to ask if I'd ever tasted coffee before, which I hadn't.

She set an empty cup and saucer in front of me and turned the cup right side up. "Cream and sugar are right here on the counter beside the carafe of ice water." She started to get the coffee.

"Could I have a glass of milk instead?"

"Certainly, Miss," she said, not a bit perturbed by me changing my mind. She stepped back, picked up my empty cup, turned it upside down, and set it next to the saucer on the counter. "Milk it is."

I watched her move down the row of customers. Several had taken seats as they came available. She took about ten drink orders and didn't write a one down.

Another Harvey Girl in rustling black-and-white stopped to ask, "May I take your order, Miss?"

"That other girl took it."

"Yes, Miss. She took your drink order. What would you like to eat?" She said it pleasant-like.

"I, uh . . ." I looked around to see what the people on either side had on their plates.

"Maybe you'd like more time to see a menu," she said. She politely handed me the one that had been on the counter all the time. I took it and thanked her, trying to hide my embarrassment as she moved on to another customer.

I had barely glanced at the menu when the first girl came back carrying a tray of drinks. She started with me and set a tall glass of milk at my place. She stepped down to the next person and gave her iced tea. She served another a small teapot of hot water and a tea bag. She set the tray down. Then one at a time, she drew five cups of coffee from the nearest gleaming urn and delivered them to customers. How did she remember all those orders?

I sipped the cool, rich milk that tasted as good as what I'd had at Granny 'hite's.

Then I read the menu. Blue points on half shell, Hungarian goulash, Vienna meat loaf with poulette of June peas, persillade potatoes, cream of new peas aux croutons, baked oysters a l'ancienne, jumbo frog legs au beurre noir. The plate dinners cost from sixty to eighty cents, so I settled on pie. It was fifteen cents, and I didn't think Opal would mind loaning me that much more.

The second girl came back to take my order. "What may I bring you?"

"A slice of apple pie."

"Certainly, Miss."

"Wait," I said as she turned to go.

Immediately, she faced me again. "I just want to ask you about my cousin."

She tilted her head.

"My cousin . . . she's a Harvey Girl. Her name is Opal Wilhite. Do you know where she is?"

"Why, no, Miss. There are hundreds of Harvey Girls."

"She works here," I said. "Opal Wilhite."

I could tell she wanted to be helpful. "I'm sorry."

An impatient man down the counter asked for more coffee.

"I'll be right with you, sir," she told him pleasantly. Then she whispered, "We're only allowed to talk to customers about their orders. Our manager has strict rules." Her eyes darted toward the man talking to the cashier.

I saw that the manager was the man who had shown me to my seat.

In a loud voice accompanied by a wink, she asked, "May I take your order, Miss?" Lowering her voice again, she said, "I'll ask the girls in the kitchen if they know your cousin."

She selected a large piece of apple pie from a pastry case, set it in front of me, and made sure I had a fork. Then she headed toward the swinging doors.

I ate the pie slowly, savoring every delicious morsel and trying not to remember the sickening slice I'd forced down at the Springfield depot.

I'd almost finished when I noticed a Harvey Girl at the far end of the counter attempting to get my attention. She gave me a quick wave, glanced across the room toward the entrance where the manager now stood, then waved again. I strained to see, and sure enough, it was Opal. I stood up to go to her. But she shook her head and motioned for me to stay in my seat. That's when I noticed the frown on her face. I sat back on the swivel seat.

The girl who had waited on me hustled out through the swinging doors and down the counter. Two customers wanted desserts. Four wanted more coffee. Three ordered off the menu. In a cranky voice, the lady on my left complained about her food. The Harvey girl told her she was sorry. She offered to take the food back, even though it was half eaten by then, and bring her another meal. But the lady said that would make her miss her train and insisted she shouldn't be charged full price.

The girl patiently explained that the woman would have to speak to the manager. The lady grumbled more, claiming she didn't have time to talk to anyone else. She left saying she would not leave a tip.

I would have told her to keep her old tip, but the Harvey Girl smiled and never said a harsh word.

After the lady left, she cleared away the lady's dirty dishes and fixed the counter for the next customer. "I found your cousin," she whispered. " I told her you were here."

"She waved at me," I said. "But she didn't come over to say hello."

"The manager wouldn't approve of her leaving her station," she said. "Your cousin wants you to wait right here until this shift is over in about an hour."

"Thanks." I drank the rest of my milk, and she cleared away my dishes, too. "How much do I owe you?"

"Your cousin said she'd settle the check."

"Do you like being a Harvey Girl?" I asked.

"Oh yes." She moved away to wait on customers, and then returned. "I love it! It's exciting. Last week I waited on Charlie Chaplin."

"The movie star? The Tramp?" The Tramp was the character the famous comedian played on the silent screen. He wore a derby hat, carried a bamboo cane, and shuffled along in shoes that were too big.

She nodded. "He sat three seats over from where you're sitting." She pointed at the swivel seat, which was now occupied by a little boy.

I couldn't believe she could calmly describe such an exciting event. "You waited on Charlie Chaplin? The funniest man in the world?"

"The very same. He ordered our Filet Mignon of Beef a la Stanley and left a dollar tip."

I had no idea what that was, but it sounded nice the way she said it.

"A dollar? Opal says she usually gets dime tips." I thought of all the dimes she had in the train case I'd brought.

"The manager's watching." The friendly waitress hurried off to serve more meals.

I looked over the menu, wondering if I should give up my seat. There were fewer customers than before and several seats were empty, so I stayed.

While I sat waiting for Opal to finish her shift, I watched the Harvey Girls bustling about the lunchroom. Even when there weren't many customers, they stayed busy. They polished the coffee urns and made fresh coffee. They folded napkins and set the tables along the wall with fresh tablecloths and silverware. At the counter, they refilled the salt and pepper shakers, the sugar bowls, and the water bottles. And they smiled. I got down off the swivel seat and stretched when I saw Opal walking toward me. I practiced my smile and stood up straight. That shift was over, and girls who looked fresh and rested took the places of my cousin and the others.

"I'm so glad to see you, Opal." I reached out to give her a hug.

But she drew back. "I wish I could say the same about you!" she said. "What are you doing here?"

I was taken aback. "I brought your train case," I said, pointing to it on the floor.

"You needn't have done that." She raised one eyebrow. I could see she was holding in her anger, probably not wanting to flare up at me in the lunchroom in front of the manager and the girls she worked with. "Do your folks know where you are?"

"No," I admitted. She'd find out if I tried to fib.

"Does that mean that you've run away from home?"

"Opal, I had to."

"What you've done is irresponsible, Clara. I thought you had better sense. Your mother is probably worried sick about you." She paused to take a deep breath.

"Opal, you don't understand."

"No, Clara, you're the one who doesn't understand. In the morning, I'm putting you back on the train. You're going home!"

7

Looking Eighteen

"I'll give you the money for the train ticket home," Opal repeated as soon as I woke up.

"I won't take any more of your money," I said, continuing the argument from the night before.

"You're getting on that train today!" She sat up in her bed and began to brush her dark, shoulder-length hair the usual one hundred strokes.

"I'm not going back!" I told her from the other bed. It belonged to her roommate, who had been obliging enough to sleep down the hall in another girl's room.

"Yes, you are!"

"I am not!" I punched my pillow up against the wrought iron headboard. "And you can't make me!"

I leaned back, crossed my arms, and stretched out my long legs, pointing my toes. It was good to have some space after sitting cramped on the train all those hours.

"You haven't finished school."

"I can't. Even if I went back. Dad, for sure, wouldn't let me now, after what I've done."

She was quiet.

"Opal, you've got to let me stay. Please!"

"Fourteen is so young, Clara." She brushed her hair full of static 'til it flew out from her head in a wide circle. "I was eighteen when I came to the city. I didn't have an easy time of it. I was straight off the farm, like you. I know what's ahead of you. Your age is against you. If you go home now and come back in four years, you'll have a much better chance of making a go of it on your own." She laid down her brush and smoothed her hair with her hands.

"Opal, I *dare* you to let me stay and get a job."

"Aha!" she said, picking up her brush and waving it at me. "You just proved my point. You're still a little kid. Talking about dares." She was quiet for a few seconds, then she laughed. "Remember the time you dared me to jump off the bluff into the swimming hole on the Jacks Fork?"

"I remember the yellow streak, running down your back. I can see it from over here."

Above the river I'd taunted and teased her while Duey Bandy "cluck, cluck, clucked," calling her chicken. We all knew about the danger. Kids had been crippled jumping into the river. Some got tangled in rootwads. Others landed in shallow water and broke bones. If any grown-ups had been on the river that day, we would have deserved a good whipping.

Still, we kept on, and finally she jumped off that high bluff into the shoulder-deep water. I laughed and hooted. Then Duey pushed me off, and he jumped in, too. The three of us played like river otters, splashing and shoving, chasing and dunking each other, and laughing 'til our sides ached.

"You always were spunky," Opal said, hopping out of bed onto the oval rug. "Well, get up! The least I can do is give you a makeover. You need one whether you go for an interview or not. Go take a bath. And wash your hair! Twice! Use my Castile soap. It's next to the tub. Be sure to rinse it a long time so it will shine. Then open up that new toothbrush that's beside the sink. And brush your teeth with salt."

Orders! Opal was as bad as my dad. But I didn't mind doing as she said.

Back in the bedroom, I found that Opal was gone, along with the mud-splattered traveling suit and the shoes I'd worn on the train. She'd threatened to burn them. I dug around in my straw valise and came up with some underthings and put them on. I laid out another of Grandma Massie's dresses and did what I could to smooth out the wrinkles. It was all I had to wear to an interview. The thought of how out-of-date I'd look answering questions in that dress made my face flush.

As I sat in front of the steam heat radiator to comb my wet, tangled hair, I admired Opal's shared room. On the two single beds were knobby, white bedspreads. Two chests of drawers stood against the opposite wall. The oak floor was polished to a shine, and lacy curtains shaded the window. In the open closet hung lots of nice dresses—stylish ones—and several black-and-white uniforms, all clean and pressed alongside a row of starched white pinafores. A dozen pair of shoes lined the closet floor. Most were pumps. Some were the sensible, black shoes that completed the Harvey Girl uniform.

On the inside of the closet door was a mirror. When I stood far enough back, I could see my whole tall self. Too bad I wasn't closer to Opal's size so I could wear her pretty things. The comfortable room gave me a nice feeling. With the rats all pulled out of my hair, I fluffed it out to dry quicker. Then I padded around the room, admiring Opal's belongings. On top of her chest lay a gold necklace with matching earrings, three tiny bottles of cologne, a brush, a comb, a hand mirror, and some fashion magazines. I picked up a magazine and lounged on the bed. I turned the pages full of pretty frocks and read the captions under the photos.

When I leafed through to the end of the magazine, my eye caught on the name *Fred Harvey* in an advertisement:

WANTED

Young women, 18 to 30 years of age, of good moral character, attractive and intelligent, as waitresses in the Harvey Eating Houses on the Santa Fe Railroad in the West. Good wages with room and meals furnished. Liberal tips customary. Experience not necessary.

Write Fred Harvey, Union Depot, Kansas City, Mo.

I read it again and again, trying to reassure myself.

"Good moral character." Unless they counted sassin' your dad and running away from home a crime, I wouldn't have a problem with that requirement.

"Intelligent." I'd finished halfway through the eighth reader. That was better than a lot of girls.

"Attractive." Well, I was certainly no Hollywood vamp. So I'd only pass that part if the interviewer considered my plain looks pleasing enough.

"Young women, 18 to 30." My stomach knotted up. Why couldn't they have stopped after the "young" part? A girl had to be eighteen to apply. So that's why Opal said to wait until I was older. I was four whole years away from living my dream as a Harvey Girl. The ad might just have read, "Clara Massie, go back to the farm!"

"Did you think I'd gotten lost?" Opal asked as she opened the door and carried in two pair of shoes under one arm and two dresses on hangers folded over the other. She dropped the shoes on the floor and laid the dresses across the bed.

I pointed at the magazine. "Opal, now I see why you said my age was against me."

Opal put her hands on her hips and gave me a disgusted, didn't-I-tell-you? look. "Harvey Girls have to be eighteen, Clara."

"Or look eighteen," I added quickly. "I'm tall and have big feet."

"Yes, you've got height and size going for you."

"I can act older, too." My voice was a bit too squeaky.

"You don't sound any more confident than I feel about that," she said.

She glanced at the clock. "We are running out of time. I've got to get ready first before I start your makeover." She didn't say a word while she dressed. I tried to think what I was going to do if the clothes she'd borrowed didn't fit. But I couldn't concentrate. I closed my eyes and saw myself trudging down our dirt road back to the farm.

When I opened them again, Opal was standing by the bed. She was dressed in her uniform, and her hair was combed back into a bun all nice and neat. She was pinning on her badge and shaking her head. I could see she thought it was no use even trying to dress me up for an interview.

I had to do something that would make her give me that makeover. I let out a loud noise. "Cluck, cluck, cluck. . . . Cluck, cluck, cluck. . . ." I wasn't as good at it as Duey Bandy, but Opal knew I was calling her a chicken.

I don't know how long I kept it up, but she finally busted out laughing. We both giggled for the longest time.

After a while, though, she managed to control herself. "Clara, I don't think you're one bit funny!"

As soon as she said it, we started laughing again. Tears welled up in my eyes, and I wiped them away with the corner of the sheet. I sat up and faced her.

"Opal, I have to get a job. I know I'm too young, but that's not going to stop me from trying. Hasn't there ever been a Harvey Girl younger than eighteen?"

She didn't answer.

"There has, hasn't there!" I clapped my hands in glee. "You know one, don't you?"

"One girl I worked with out in Barstow was only fourteen."

"And she did okay?"

Opal seemed reluctant to tell. "Well, for a while. Then she got fired."

"Because she was too young?"

"No, she came in after the curfew three times, and the manager fired her."

"How did she get hired in the first place?" I asked.

"Fibbed. Which is what you'll have to do. When Miss Steel—she does all the interviewing—when she asks how old you are, fib!"

I'd never been very good at fibbing. And I knew it was wrong. But what would become of me if I didn't try?

"Stand up," Opal said, suddenly in a hurry. "And put these on."

She handed me a girdle, a pair of black stockings, and a garter out of her top drawer. I gave her a big grin and slipped my legs into the girdle, stood on the oval rug, and began the tortuous struggle that Opal claimed every woman suffered through to look fashionable. I pulled and squirmed, pulled and wriggled my hips, and pulled again 'til I finally had the thing snugged around my middle. I could barely breathe, but my tummy was flat as a griddle cake. Then I put on the stockings, nearly stretching a hole in the toes. I pulled them up just below my knees and rolled them over the garters.

Opal found another undergarment in her drawer. "It's a camisole. It will flatten you out on the top and give you the debutante look."

It did.

"Good. Right in style." Making me over was serious business to her. "I borrowed these dresses from a tall girl down the hall," Opal said.

She held them up, then handed me the pale yellow one without letting me choose. I liked the maroon one better. I started to protest, then decided not to do anything that might cause her to quit helping me. I pulled the long jersey over my head and gazed at my slim figure in the closet mirror. The dress fell to about midcalf, and the tight undergarments left me with no bosom and no waistline. I pushed my big feet into the pumps she had borrowed. They were snug, but they fit better than my old shoes. For the first time in my life, I wore the latest fashion.

"Sit on the bed," she told me. "I'll comb your hair in the Harvey Girl style."

She parted it down the middle, brushed it back away from my face, and pinned it in a loose knot at the back.

"Perfect," she claimed. "You look fresh-scrubbed and proper, the way the Harvey people like. No makeup. Don't chew gum during the interview. And smile."

I obeyed.

"Round your shoulders forward like a debutante."

I slouched as best I could, but I still rose to almost six feet in those pumps.

"You look eighteen," she said. "There isn't a soul around who'd ever believe you're only fourteen—unless you tell. Which you're not going to do. It's not like anyone can tell your age by looking at your teeth like they do a horse."

"They look better now, don't they?" I grinned so she could see my teeth.

"Much better," she said. "And you can keep that toothbrush. Use it every day."

Opal ran a hand down her starched pinafore. Then she warned me. "You have to get hired today. That's the only way you'll have a place to live. You can't stay here another night because if you get caught, we'll both be on our way back to the farm."

The evening before, after we tiptoed down the corridor of the boarding house to her room, Opal had warned me not to go back out unless she made sure the coast was clear. She said the overseer of the girls stuck strictly to the Harvey rules, and no guests—especially no men—were allowed in the girls' rooms.

"Tell me what to do in the interview," I demanded.

"Shut your mouth!"

"You don't have to yell at me, Opal."

"No, I mean, that's the answer. You have to shut your mouth during the interview."

"I have to answer questions, don't I?"

"Of course, but you don't have to ramble on. Answer with a simple 'yes' or 'no.' Be polite and smile."

I listened to Opal's instructions about how to get to the Fred Harvey Company's main office, which was in Union Station. I walked with her as far as the lunchroom, doing the best I could to stay steady in those borrowed pumps.

"Do you want to eat some breakfast?" she asked.

I shook my head. "I can't while I'm wearing this girdle."

She giggled. "If you are going to be a Harvey Girl, you'll have to get used to it. It's part of the uniform."

As she went to start her shift, I thanked her for everything she'd done. Then I set out on my own.

Smile, I told myself, and did. A gentleman coming toward me in the crowd of passengers tipped his hat.

Could I really pass for eighteen?

8

Pretty Waiter Girls

When I entered the business offices of the Fred Harvey Company, a stiff-backed secretary glanced up from the shorthand notes beside her Remington, but she continued typing.

Forcing my best smile, I wobbled over to her desk on my borrowed pumps. My underarms were moist, and my knees knocked together. Two girls, older than me by several years, sat in the middle of a row of wooden chairs lining the wall. I could feel their eyes appraising my dress, my hairdo, my tall body, my extralong feet, and my smile.

My throat clogged with nervousness. I cleared it, hoping the clatter of the Remington's keys would cover the sound. At that moment, the secretary lifted her fingers away from the keyboard. My half-cough filled the sudden silence.

With a stern look above the rim of her glasses, the secretary upbraided me, "Be patient, young lady." She placed the most emphasis on *young*.

I muttered, "Sorry," but she shushed me as the door to the inner office opened. All eyes in the room focused on a redheaded girl close to my age. Accompanying her was a short, balding man, politely carrying his felt hat. They crossed the room to the outside door.

"Thank you, ma'am," the man said to the secretary as he held the door for the girl. "We're on our way to the seamstress so Nellie can be fitted for her uniform."

The redhead smiled at the woman, too. "Yes, thank you very much." Her eyes were the azure color of a Missoura spring. I imagined how pretty she would be in Harvey Girl black-and-white.

The secretary said pleasantly, "Welcome to the Fred Harvey Company."

After they left, one of the girls sitting by the wall whispered to the other, "Can you believe she got hired?"

"I wonder who answered all the questions in the interview," the other girl said bitterly. "Her or her daddy?"

In a louder voice, the first girl added, "I don't think it's fair. If a girl can't apply on her own, she shouldn't get a job."

The secretary ignored them and looked at me.

Thinking she expected me to speak up, I blurted out, "I want to be a Harvey Girl!"

Both eavesdropping girls snickered.

The secretary frowned. "Do you have an appointment?"

I shook my head, remembering the advertisement I'd read in the magazine that morning back in Opal's room. It said to *write* to the Fred Harvey Company.

"My cousin didn't tell me you'uns would require an appointment."

One of the girls whispered, "Listen to that hayseed. She'll never get a job with Fred Harvey."

I felt my face heat up.

The secretary pulled out a desk drawer and handed me a form. "Fill out this application. Don't leave any blanks." As I took it, she asked, "Do you have a fountain pen?"

"Not with me," I said apologetically. "I could go and get one from my cousin."

"I'll loan you one," she said curtly, pointing to one on her desk. "Just be sure you don't walk off with it! Sit over there."

I picked up the fountain pen and chose a seat in the row of chairs, four down from the two girls.

"What's the matter?" one of them asked. She chewed her gum, popping it twice.

Then her friend, who looked unnatural in her bright rouge and red lipstick, said. "Leave her be, Mabel. We don't want to catch nothing. You know how it is with girls straight off the farm."

"How is it?" her friend said, popping her gum again.

"They're crawling with chiggers and ticks." They guffawed.

Embarrassed, I fumbled with the fountain pen and stared down at the application. I blinked away the moisture that blurred my vision and began to answer the questions. I laid the paper on my lap and tried printing my name as the directions said. But the fountain pen wouldn't work. I gave it a good shake and pressed down harder against my leg, punching a hole right through the paper. A dot of black ink leaked onto the pale yellow of the borrowed dress.

I had no idea how to remove ink from jersey cloth. If I got the job, I'd have to save enough money from my wages to have the dress properly laundered. If I didn't get it, I'd have to borrow more money from Opal.

I was puzzling over how to fill out the form when the secretary called out, "Mabel Taylor, Miss Steel will see you now."

The gum-chewing girl stood up. "Wish me luck," she said to her friend.

"Honey, you won't need it," the other girl assured her. "With your experience! Why, if that Miss Steel don't hire you, she's got rocks . . ." She interrupted herself to giggle. "I take it back. She's got steel nuggets in her head."

With a confident smile, Mabel Taylor pranced off to the inner office.

I picked up a *Santa Fe Railway* magazine from a nearby end table and placed it on my lap between the application form and the yellow dress. In the top blank, I carefully printed my name, then filled in my age: 18. I mentally repeated it—18—to make sure I wouldn't forget.

I used Granny 'hite's place for my home address. Two fibs, I realized guiltily. But it wouldn't do to leave an easy way for my dad to find out what I was up to.

I put Opal's and Miss Forester's names down in the blanks for references. But I didn't know what to write in the space for previous experience. I'd never had a job. I felt a queasiness that wasn't caused by having my empty stomach squeezed inside some other girl's tight clothes. Carefully, I laid the fountain pen down on the chair next to me.

It must have been the frown on my face that made the rouged girl start talking again.

"What's the matter, honey?" she asked in a syrupy tone. "You never had a job?"

I shook my head, but quickly added. "I read an advertisement for Harvey Girls. It said experience wasn't necessary." I didn't sound as confident as I had hoped, though.

The girl's bright red lips parted in a sneer. "Yeah, I've heard that. But don't believe everything you hear. That's one important thing I've learned the hard way." She sounded sure.

I felt like I was swimming against the strong current in the river.

"Now you take me and Mabel," the girl said in a chatty voice. "We've got lots of experience for our nineteen years."

My eyes widened. She was younger than Opal. But why did she look so much older? So haggard?

"We had plenty of jobs in California," she went on. "Until laws were passed saying women couldn't waitress in establishments serving liquor. Then Prohibition did the rest. Full-time jobs got hard to find. Some people, believe it or not, look down on a girl who has worked in a place that serves whiskey."

I knew my dad would. I concentrated on the application form again. The blank space, where other girls would list all the jobs they'd had, loomed larger than before.

Mabel's friend chattered away. "So me and Mabel worked part-time for a while. Then we hopped a train and came here to apply for positions with the Harvey Company. It won't be as exciting as what we're used to, but they say tips are good. They give you a nice room to stay in and all the food you can eat. And the railroad men, as I'm sure you've heard . . ."—she leaned toward me and lowered her voice—". . . are the marrying kind."

She grinned. "Mabel claims a brakeman or a fireman will suit her fine. But I've got my heart set on a conductor. There's nothing finer than a man in a blue serge uniform."

I stared at her.

"Oh, don't fret, honey. There's plenty of men to go around."

"But I-I-I need the job to support myself," I stammered. "I don't want to get married."

"After a few years, you'll be tired of working, honey, like me. Then you'll wish you had a man to take care of you."

She did look tired—worn out, actually. But when I thought of my dad and what my momma put up with being married to him, I said, "I don't want a husband if he's anything like my dad."

The girl looked at me more kindly, but she said, "At least you know who your dad is. Mabel's little girl will never know hers. He died fighting in Germany."

Before I could say anything, she went back to talking about how sure she was that she'd soon be a Harvey Girl.

"Another thing me and Mabel have in our favor," she said, "is there are two of us."

"What do you mean?" I asked.

"They like to hire two girls together. So many of the young ones, like yourself, get homesick and quit. The management figures that two girls who are friends won't be so lonesome. Two friends are more likely to finish out their contracts." She ended on a laugh. "If they don't get married first."

The queasiness in my stomach turned into an ache. I'd never get a job as a Harvey Girl. But I might get one in a factory, I thought, in an effort to reassure myself, sewing uniforms or assembling airplane parts, like lots of girls did during the war. I should be spending my time finding out what kinds of factory jobs there were for a girl like me in Kansas City. I felt very glum.

When Mabel came out of Miss Steel's office, I didn't look up until I heard her angry voice.

"Well, I never!" she fumed.

Her rouged friend joined her in front of the secretary's desk. "Didn't you get hired?"

"That woman insulted me." She pointed her finger toward the inner office. "When I told her about all the places I'd worked, she thanked me for coming, but said Fred Harvey wasn't looking for pretty waiter girls whose experience was in saloons."

"She called you a pretty waiter girl!"

"Like I was low class. She said I didn't measure up to Harvey standards."

"Well, I certainly don't want this job if they didn't hire you," her friend said. "Come on. Let's find an establishment where we'll be appreciated."

They were out the door in a huff.

I was more stunned than they were. If they hadn't gotten hired with their experience, what chance did a farm girl have with no experience at all?

9

No Experience Necessary

I sat rigidly on the hard chair as the secretary pounded the keys of her Remington. After several fidgety minutes, I folded the application and headed for the door. As I passed the secretary's desk, I returned her pen.

She quit typing and eyed me. "Have you completed your application?" She reached out to take it. "I'll give it to Miss Steel so she can look it over before she sees you."

I couldn't admit I was trying to escape. I gave it to her.

"You may sit down again until she's ready."

Dumbly, I stared after her as she carried the form into the inner office. I looked at the outside door. I could be gone before she came back.

Nobody but Opal would know. And I could just hear her. "Cluck, cluck, cluck." She'd have a grand time calling me a chicken and demanding to see the yellow stripe down *my* back. Which was worse? Being humiliated by some woman I'd never see again? Or facing my cousin?

I went back to the row of wooden chairs, sat down, and stared at my lap. The ink stain had spread. Instead of being a dot, it was now a circle half an inch wide. I rested my clammy palms across it, trying to hold my hands to hide the blob.

"Clara Massie," the secretary said, returning from the inner office, "Miss Steel is ready to see you."

I stood up very tall. I forced a big smile and went to face Miss Steel.

In her office, I sat on the edge of the chair in front of her huge mahogany desk and hid the ink blob with one hand. From the stacks of folders on the desk to the leather-bound books in a glass case, everything was citified, businesslike, and neat.

That included middle-aged Miss Steel behind her desk in a dark gray suit. Her short, wavy hair framed her face like a fashionable brown hat.

"Clara Fern Massie? It's nice to meet you." She sounded genuinely pleased.

I nodded, remembering to keep my mouth shut.

"Your application looks good."

Did she mean that?

"I have several questions for you."

"I hope I know all the answers, ma'am. I didn't know what to study on."

Amused, she said, "The questions are all about you, Clara. Just answer honestly."

That made me nervous.

She looked at my application. "You turned eighteen on your last birthday?"

Was I to start with a fib?

She looked up, not waiting for my answer. "When was your birthday?"

I could answer that truthfully. "A week ago yesterday."

"Happy birthday," she said.

"Thank you," I managed a faint smile, recalling what a nightmare that day that had been.

"Tell me about your schooling, Clara."

I didn't mind answering what I was proud of. "I finished over halfway through the eighth reader. And my teacher said I was the best scholar in the school. I studied hard."

I realized suddenly I'd been talking with my hands, waving them about. I slapped them back down over the ink stain.

"I like book learning. Miss Forester hoped I could move over to West Eminence and attend high school."

"Why didn't you go on to high school, Clara?"

"I'm not . . ." Old enough skidded to a stop at the tip of my tongue. My heart pounded with the near slip. Then I had to explain myself. "The honest-to-gosh truth is, my dad, he thinks going to school puts fancy ideas into a girl's head. Causes her to get above her raising. He never finished the first reader himself." My palms sweated on the jersey dress.

"I see," she said, looking like she was truly interested in my words. "Tell me about the rest of your family, Clara."

"Well, my momma works hard, tending to the chickens and making butter and doing all the chores. I help her with the washing and ironing and canning."

"Do you have any brothers or sisters?"

"Bobby Earl is the youngest. Seven and a half. Alice is nine. Then there's me. And Beulah is the oldest."

"How old is she?"

I had to think quick. I couldn't say her real age—sixteen. If I was eighteen, and Beulah was the oldest . . . "She's two years older than me. Twenty."

One little fib led to another. And it was hard to keep track.

"What is Beulah doing now?"

At my puzzled look, she asked, "Is she still living at home? Married? Working?"

"Oh, no, Beulah isn't able to do for herself. She's been afflicted since her girlhood."

"Afflicted?"

"She fell out of the loft when she was little. Granny 'hite says she has tuberculosis of the spine. She can't walk or use her right arm. We all help her as best we can."

"An invalid."

I nodded.

"How very sad. That means your sister will need special care all her life."

"Why, yes, I suppose so." I hadn't thought of it that way.

"Which places an extra burden on you, doesn't it? You will need to work and support yourself. Perhaps even share the expense of caring for your sister at some point."

"Oh, Miss Steel, I would surely like to do that."

My thinking had never reached far enough into the future to include sharing my wages with my family. But I liked the idea. Maybe my dad would get over being sore at me for running off if I could send some money home.

"Why do you want to work as a Harvey Girl?"

"It will be more exciting than clerking in a dime store," I said without thinking.

Miss Steel's eyes narrowed slightly, and she seemed to be trying not to smile.

"Any other reason?" she asked.

"My cousin Opal is a Harvey Girl. And she likes it fine. She gets to travel and meet lots of nice people and save her wages."

Miss Steel's face lit up. "Where is your cousin now?"

"Here in Union Station at the lunch counter. She's been a Harvey Girl for two years. And she's worked in California and Arizona. And at the Grand Canyon as an extra girl for a month."

"Marvelous."

"I know Opal will put in a good word for me," I said, pointing to my application. "I wrote her name down."

"We're always pleased to hire the younger sister, or other relative, of one of our girls. It seems they have a better chance of success. You have some big shoes to fill."

"I know," I said. "My momma calls my size nines a good understanding." I lifted my big feet in the borrowed black pumps.

Miss Steel laughed. "And a natural sense of humor is a plus in a Harvey Girl, too." Then she went on in a serious tone. "Being a Harvey Girl isn't easy, Clara. It's hard work."

"I'm stout."

"If I hire you, your first position will be far away from home. Can you cope with homesickness?"

I nodded, but didn't say what I was thinking—being homesick would be easier to take than going home.

"I have an opening in Belen. It's a pleasant little town in the middle of New Mexico. Its Harvey House is not as grand as the Alvarado in Albuquerque or the Casteñada farther up the line. But I've found it best to send our youngest and greenest girls to a small place for their training. Would you be willing to start in Belen?"

"Oh, yes, ma'am. I'd be proud to."

"Are you available to board the train tonight and head for New Mexico?"

"I sure could." I kept my mouth shut about not having any other place to sleep. "All I need to do is tell Opal where I'm going."

"I must warn you that the training period is rigorous. Some girls have compared it to being in the army."

"I'm used to farm chores."

She gave me a doubtful look. "Being a Harvey Girl is very different from farm life. You must learn the Harvey way. That includes setting a proper table, keeping the silver polished, efficiently serving hot meals to trainloads of weary passengers three or four times a day, and following all the strict Harvey rules."

"I'll do my best."

"You must sign a six-month contract, agreeing not to marry during that time."

"I'm too young to get married," I blurted out before I could stop myself. Then I held my breath. Had I ruined everything?

"I'm glad you feel that way, Clara. Too many of our girls marry too young. Wait until you are in your twenties."

I let out my breath slow and easy, relieved, but determined not to make another mistake. Excitement was building inside me.

"And you must wear a smile and a starched, spotless uniform."

Spotless.

I'd forgotten to keep my hand over the ink blob. When I tried to cover it up again, Miss Steel looked right at it.

"Oh my," she said. "That's a bad stain on such a lovely dress. How did it happen?"

"I borrowed a fountain pen from your secretary and it leaked." I stopped, wishing I could take back my words. "But I'm not blaming her. It was my own fault. My dad says I'm clumsy on account of being tall."

I stopped talking when I saw the pitying look in her eyes. Why hadn't I taken Opal's advice not to talk too much?

"That's a shame," Miss Steel said.

"Oh, I'll grow out of my clumsiness," I told her.

"I'm sure you will," she said, leaning back in her chair. "Have your cousin send that dress to our laundry with her uniforms. The cleaning bill's on Fred Harvey."

"Thank you, ma'am. And thank you for giving me a chance to get above my raising."

"I like your spunk, Clara. You are perhaps a trifle young, but you have a fresh scrubbed look—no makeup, no jewelry. And you're not chewing gum. We prefer to hire girls with no experience. That way, we can train them properly."

I kept my mouth closed tight. Then she handed over the contract for me to sign.

After she gave me instructions about getting fitted for my uniform, she said, "We like for our girls to travel two by two. Before you board the train at midnight, look for a girl with red hair. Introduce yourself and stay together. I've assigned you both to the Belen Harvey House."

Then she issued me my railroad pass.

"Ma'am," I said, standing up. "I'll work hard to prove you didn't do the wrong thing by giving me this job."

"I don't often make mistakes, Clara," she said. "I've hired many a green country girl who has become a poised young woman after completing one contract with us."

"You mean it's possible to turn a sow's ear into a silk purse?"

After Miss Steel quit laughing, she said, "It certainly is."

10

Go West, Young Woman!

We rolled along in a modern passenger car of the Atchison, Topeka, and Santa Fe. Mile after desolate mile, metal wheels clicked against steel rails. I had become used to the machinelike rhythm and the odor of formaldehyde in the car. One of the conductors told me and Nellie Baker, the pretty redhead Miss Steel had hired a few minutes before she hired me, that the smell was "standard train equipment" and "free of charge." I took him to be serious until I saw Nellie's grin.

That friendly conductor in the blue serge uniform was on the crew out of Wichita, Kansas, as I recalled. It wasn't easy to remember. On the two-day trip, the railroad crews had changed so many times I'd lost count.

"They're sending you to the Horny Toad!" that conductor said when Nellie mentioned we were new Harvey Girls headed for the Belen Harvey House.

"The Horny Toad?" I repeated.

He laughed. "That's what railroad men call the segment of the railway from Albuquerque to El Paso. Belen is on that part of the Santa Fe line."

Visions formed in my head—giant toads with horns as long as the ones we had seen on the steers along the track. Were they real or just a tall tale, like the gowrows in the Ozarks? Was that conductor lying to us strangers?

"How did it get the name Horny Toad?" I wanted to know.

"Back in the early days of the railroad, so many horny toads covered the tracks that crews stayed busy sweeping them off to keep the trains' wheels from slipping."

"How big are these toads?"

His grin made me wish I hadn't asked. But he showed me with his fist that they were the size of normal toad frogs.

"Don't worry. It's not the horny toads you'll need to shoo away. It's the Horny Toad Men. They're *mucho hombre*, a lot of man, and they are partial to Harvey Girls. You two will get plenty of invitations to shows and dances, not to mention marriage proposals."

He'd included me when he said, "You two," but his eyes were on Nellie.

"I would never shoo them away," Nellie whispered after the conductor had moved on down the aisle.

I reminded her of the contracts we had signed, promising not to marry. "It's against the rules for Harvey Girls to even date Fred Harvey employees."

"But not railroad men. They work for the Atchison, Topeka, and Santa Fe Railway, not for Fred Harvey."

Even nicer than the conductors were the Harvey Girls who served us along the way. About every hundred miles, the train stopped at a depot. While the railroad men attended to the needs of the steam engine, the passengers disembarked, during the daylight hours, for a twenty-minute break to eat breakfast, lunch, or dinner at a Harvey House. Every eatery was as elegant as the last whether in downtown Topeka or in the desert of New Mexico.

Nellie and I watched everything those Harvey Girls did from taking orders to assisting the manager serve in the dining room. When the conductor called, "Bo-a-r-r-r-d!" we scurried back to our seats and started telling each other all we'd noticed. We spent the most time guessing how many dime tips the passengers left underneath their saucers. It was like counting your chickens before they hatch, dreaming of the tips that would soon be ours.

After one stop, I said, "The hardest part of the job is going to be remembering the orders. Did you notice that the girls don't write them on a pad?"

Nellie nodded. "I saw that, but it won't be the hardest part for me." she said. "Carrying those big trays loaded with plates of food and full glasses will be."

I was glad I was strong. I bested Nellie's height by a good four inches, and her weight by . . . well, let's just say I would not be able to fit into her uniforms, lengthwise or waistwise.

After we had been hired in Kansas City, we had been fitted for uniforms. The seamstress who fitted Nellie assured her that uniforms in her size had already been made up. They would be shipped on the next train west. But I was told my uniforms would take about a week to get to Belen.

After we left the Vaughn Harvey House, the last one before we arrived in Belen, Nellie snoozed, leaning back on our plush green velvet bench seat.

I gazed out the window. That part of the West was surely the most desolate place on earth. It reminded me of back in Missoura where the trees had been clear-cut. But it was much worse. It looked as though nothing had ever grown there. Or ever would.

The land was dry. There were no rivers or springs. Windmills, with their fan blades spinning in the blowing dust, stood every few miles in a vast, empty land of straw-colored grass. They pumped water from underground into storage tanks.

Cattle grazed, backs to the wind. Antelope started in the opposite direction at the sound of the train. And telegraph poles lined the tracks. I never saw a farmhouse in any of those miles.

I perked up when we passed some ponds that reflected the sun like the iced-over mill pond where I skated every winter. But I heard the father in the seat behind me tell his boys, "They're salt lakes, not ponds, and the water is not fit for drinking any more than ocean water is. A lot of the soil out West is alkali."

On the horizon, the outline of hazy, purple mountains met the dome of brilliant blue sky. The sun was so bright it hurt my eyes to keep them open for long, and they ached for the softness of green grass, fog, and shade trees.

I was homesick, but not lonely. Nellie and I shared the thrill of being new Harvey Girls. When we were awake, that is. At night a porter fixed our berths in the Pullman, and we slept in first-class luxury as the train kept heading west.

We told each other about our families and our lives. At eighteen, Nellie was the oldest of five kids. Her mom had died in 1918 of the Spanish influenza like hundreds of others during the epidemic that claimed more lives than the World War had. Her father worked at a factory in Illinois. Six months before, he had married a widow woman, who had four kids of her own. That made a family of eleven mouths to feed.

Nellie didn't get along with her stepmother. Being the new wife, she thought all the household goods were hers now, even the things that had belonged to Nellie's mother.

Some were heirlooms from Scotland brought to this country by Nellie's grandmother. Nellie felt she should inherit them. Her mother had told her they would be hers someday, part of her trousseau when she was married. But her stepmother claimed them all.

A family argument started when Nellie hid some of the precious things under her bed. When her stepmother found them, there was a scene. Nellie's father took his new wife's side. So Nellie decided to leave home and get a job. She wrote the Fred Harvey Company and was told in a letter to come for an interview. Her father insisted on accompanying her to Kansas City.

Her dad sounded so nice, I was embarrassed to say I'd run away from home on account of mine. But I told her all about Alice and Bobby Earl and about Beulah's accident and her being in a wheelchair and how sick she had been all summer, coughing up blood.

"Could she have consumption?" Nellie had asked, meaning tuberculosis.

We had both seen the lungers, as the sufferers of the disease were called, riding on our train. They were going to Albuquerque for climate therapy. The hot, dry desert air and the high altitude was said to cure tuberculosis, a passenger told us.

"Granny 'hite has always claimed Beulah had tuberculosis of the spine."

"How old is Beulah?" Nellie asked.

"Sixteen," I answered without thinking. "Two years older than me."

Nellie got real quiet, and I realized what I had done. When you tell a fib, it isn't a one-time thing that you can lock up in a shadowy part of your past. You have to remember to keep fibbing over and over to every new person you meet. Otherwise, you'll be found out, or slip up, like I'd done. What you have to do is live a lie.

She broke the silence. "You're only fourteen?"

I could lie again and convince her I was really eighteen. But I was tired of lying and I thought she was my friend, so I told the truth.

"My cousin Opal helped me dress so I would look older before I went for the interview."

"She did a good job."

"Did you think I looked eighteen?"

"You had me fooled. You act younger, though. But I thought that was because you are straight off the farm."

That gave me a fright.

"I need this job," I whispered. "I can't go home."

"Your secret is safe with me," she said, reaching over to give me a reassuring pat on the arm.

Nellie woke up the minute we stopped at the Belen Harvey House. Above the noise of the train's engine, we could hear the busboy banging on the brass gong out front. He was directing passengers either to the lunch counter or to the dining room.

Nellie pointed out a man in a dark suit, welcoming passengers at the dining room entrance.

"He's probably the manager," she said.

We gathered our valises and stepped down from the gangway onto a brickyard that led up to the building. In the bright sun, I had to shade my eyes with my hand to see.

Then I didn't know where to look first—at the Indians balancing clay pots on their heads who were selling pottery and jewelry to the disembarking passengers, at the lungers who were being helped or carried off the train by nurses and doctors, at the townspeople gathered to watch the train arrive the way the local citizens all along the track had done, or at the pretty park on both sides of the Harvey House.

There in the middle of the desert was a green lawn underneath tall shade trees whose leaves hadn't yet turned their fall colors. *An oasis!* was all I could think. I didn't feel nearly as homesick then.

We were as hungry for lunch as the other passengers, but we hung back until nearly all of them had filed through the arches, across the covered porch, and into the building that resembled a Spanish mission. Then we approached the manager, a short, stocky man with a neatly trimmed mustache and goatee. His stern expression made me cautious. So I let Nellie do the talking.

"Are you the manager, sir?" She was shouting to be heard above the engine noise.

"I am," he yelled back.

"We are new Harvey Girls."

"It's about time!" he said, pulling a white handkerchief from the breast pocket of his jacket. He mopped his glistening brow and tucked the cloth neatly back into his pocket.

"I'm Mr. Phillips. You will go right to work, of course. After you change into proper uniforms."

"But, Mr. Phillips," I blurted out in my loudest voice, "my uniforms won't arrive for at least a week."

He gave me an angry look and exploded. "I won't tolerate slackers in this Harvey House!"

"It isn't my fault," I said.

"Find your room on the second floor. Change into a uniform. Borrow from the other girls if you have to! And report to the kitchen. Immediately!"

I hung my head and shut my eyes tight to block out the sun. Not five minutes on duty at my new job, and the boss was already yelling at me.

Worst of all, on our two-day trip, I had not seen another Harvey Girl as tall as me. If I was the tallest one in this house, too, there would be no uniform upstairs that was long enough to fit me properly.

Would Mr. Phillips hand me a ticket for home when I reported to the kitchen out of uniform?

11

Green as the Hills

A dark-skinned boy showed us to the back of the Harvey House through the shady park.

"I'm Estevan Chavez. I'm a call boy," he said with unmistakable pride.

When neither of us commented, he explained. "A call boy *es muy importante.*"

My puzzled expression must have assured him we didn't understand.

"I have a very important job. I call the train crews so they won't be late for their shifts."

"Call them? How?" Nellie asked with more interest than I had on the subject.

"I go to the boarding house or the reading room and tell the crews when it's time to report for duty. I know all the men of the Horny Toad."

"All of them?" Nellie asked. "Sounds like it's you, not the job, that is *muy importante.*"

He gave her a big grin as he stopped and pointed to the back entrance. "Here's the door to the Harvey Girls' dormitory."

Still carrying our valises, Nellie and I kept walking.

"Thank you," I said over my shoulder when I noticed the boy hadn't left.

"*De nada.* And don't worry about the tip," he said. "I can wait until you get paid."

Nellie nodded.

"I also deliver messages, for a slight fee," he said, more to Nellie than to me, "if either of you pretty ladies should desire to send such a message."

Nellie laughed. "Give me time to meet the right *hombre* first."

"That should not take long," he said, his dark eyes flashing. "The flame of your hair will fire the hearts of the Horny Toad men."

After he ran off, I wondered if he worked for tips *only*, the way Nellie and I would during our month of training. Of course, our meals and room were part of the contract we had signed. But our salary would not start until the second month, and then only if our work was satisfactory.

Inside the building, it took my eyes a while to adjust to the darkness. The delicious aroma of lunch tantalized me. Were we going to get another meal today? We had eaten breakfast hours before.

When I could finally see again, I knew the door in front of us must lead to the kitchen where Mr. Phillips said to report after changing into uniforms.

We started up the wooden stairs, not sure how we would know which room was ours. On the creaky landing, I looked back down as a Harvey Girl burst through the kitchen door. She took the stairs two at a time, hopping in a nimble way that reminded me of a gray squirrel. The stairs groaned as if protesting her energy.

"There you are," she said. "I was afraid you might have gotten back on the train after Mr. Phillips *welcomed* you." She said "welcomed" in a sarcastic way.

When she caught up with us on the landing, I could tell that she was older than most of the Harvey Girls I'd seen. A few streaks of gray showed along the part down the middle of her black hair.

Not a bit out of breath, she went on, "He fancies he's Fred Harvey reincarnated. Always going around wiping the silver with his handkerchief, looking for fingerprints and dust. Wants everything to be perfect in case the big Harvey bosses show up for inspection. He's a poor imitation, though, of the original Mr. Harvey, God rest his soul."

"Oh, how sad," I said. "When did he pass on?"

Nellie giggled.

The Harvey Girl explained that the original Mr. Harvey had been dead for years. His sons ran the company now.

"Are you Clara Massie?" she asked.

I told her I was and wondered how she guessed.

"Miss Steel wired that one of you was a farm girl from Missouri," she said, "and spoke with an Ozark accent."

I tried to hide my embarrassment as she greeted Nellie.

"And you must be Nellie Baker from Illinois."

Nellie smiled. "Pleased to meet you."

"I'm the headwaitress in this house. My name's Viola Vincent. Most of the girls call me Vi. Miss Vincent is too much of a mouthful." Her voice was friendly with a note of no-nonsense efficiency in it. "But I don't really care what you call me as long as you follow the Harvey rules to the letter. Any questions?"

I started to ask about lunch, but I didn't.

"We've got to find you some uniforms quickly," she went on. "I left Flora in charge of the dining room, and that makes Mr. Phillips nervous."

At the top of the stairs, she warned us about the steps. "They squeak even when you tiptoe. My room is right here across the hall. So don't try to come in after the ten o'clock curfew. I'm a light sleeper."

Under the spell of her take-charge manner, we followed her, not quite keeping up with the pace she set.

Our room was down the hall and around the corner, third door on the right, overlooking the front of the building. The noise of the engine on the tracks below left little doubt that freight trains would keep us awake at night.

There was no time to enjoy our room, or even decide which of the two beds would be mine. Several uniforms hung in the closet, and Vi said they were Nellie's.

"I'll go down the hall and see what I can scrounge up for our tall friend here. But, Nellie, you go ahead and change. And, girls, you must be properly attired."

Vi was gone before I could open my valise to get out the things I would need. She was back by the time Nellie had gotten into her black dress and reached for a starched white pinafore. I was still struggling into the girdle Opal had insisted I bring. I noticed that Nellie had not put hers on, but I didn't tattle on her.

"Not much luck," Vi said, even though she was carrying a uniform. "I could only find one that might do for a couple of shifts—if you don't spill anything on it."

"I'll be extra careful," I promised.

"We used to have a tall girl from Texas working here. But she transferred up the line to the Casteñada, and naturally all her uniforms went with her."

"The seamstress in Kansas City said mine might take a week," I said.

"Then we may have to borrow a couple from Tex. She's closer than Kansas City."

"What will I do until then?" I pictured myself washing dishes or scrubbing floors. I'd do anything *except* get back on that train and head east.

"Wear whatever we can find for the moment. Alter this uniform tonight after your shift is over. And don't let Mr. Phillips see how short it is. He'll fire you on the spot."

When I had finally wriggled into the tight girdle, I could barely breathe. Vi handed me the uniform.

"I've got to get back downstairs before something goes wrong in the dining room," she said. "Report to the kitchen as soon as possible."

We could hear her rapid steps down the hall as we hurried to don our uniforms. The black dress Vi had handed me was easy enough to get into. And it fit fairly well, except for the length. It needed to be exactly eight inches off the floor, but it was a good twelve inches. I checked the hem to see about letting it out, but there wasn't enough material to alter it much. The starched white pinafore, which was as short as the dress, could almost stand on its own, and it threatened to fight back when I tried to find a way into it.

"Let me help," Nellie offered.

It was a good thing she was there. She knew how the black bow tie went in the front of the white collar.

Then we put on hairnets and fixed our white hair ribbons. The only thing left was shoes. Nellie had nice comfortable ones. All I had were some castoffs Opal had stuffed into my straw valise. She had gotten them from a girl who said they pinched her toes. They didn't fit me either, but they were all I had until I could get a paycheck and order some that did fit or until these stretched out.

I glanced into the mirror above the vanity in the corner and tucked a strand of stray hair into my hairnet. Nellie looked terrific. Her uniform fit perfectly. Her red hair looked especially pretty in contrast to the stark black and white.

"Good luck," I told her, feeling that I needed it more than she did.

"And now," she said, "to catch that eligible man! I get dibs on the richest one."

It was funny, and I laughed, but there was also a hint of warning in her voice.

We followed our noses to the kitchen. We stood off to one side, out of the way of all the activity. Busboys carrying trays of dirty dishes, chefs in white hats ladling food into bowls, an assortment of other kitchen helpers making salad or scrubbing pots, and Harvey Girls in spotless uniforms all bustled back and forth.

We waited, wondering if Vi had forgotten us. My underarms got moist due to my nervousness and to the hot, steamy air in the room.

Finally, Vi burst through the swinging doors from the dining room. She shook her head.

"Nellie, go back up to your room and put a girdle on."

"I forgot about it in the rush," Nellie said.

How could she have forgotten when I was struggling into mine?

Then Vi turned her disapproving look on me.

"It's even shorter than I thought it would be," she said, indicating my uniform. "Behind the counter, your hem won't be as noticeable as it would be in the dining room where Mr. Phillips rides herd over the serving. I'll assign you to the part of the lunch counter where the railroad men eat."

"Nellie, you can start in the dining room—after you are properly attired."

She gave me a look of envy.

"You have all the luck," Nellie whispered.

Vi had turned to speak to Mr. Phillips, who had just walked into the kitchen. He was aiming straight toward me.

"You're fired!" Mr. Phillips shouted the minute he got close enough. "Fired! Do you hear me?"

The force of his words caused me to stagger backward and nearly stumble because of my too-tight shoes. The commotion in the kitchen stopped. Busboys, dishwashers, chefs, Harvey Girls, Vi, and Nellie—all stared at me.

"Mr. Phillips, I haven't done anything wrong," I defended myself.

"Harvey Girl uniforms are to be precisely eight inches off the floor. And I don't need a tape measure to see that yours misses that mark by many inches."

"I've already told you," I began. "My uniforms haven't arrived yet. They will be here in a week."

"A week!" he sputtered. "I can't have you traipsing around here for a whole week in an ill-fitting uniform. You cannot stay. And that's final."

"You can't fire me for being tall," I blurted out.

"I have Harvey standards to maintain," he said. Then he turned on Vi. "And don't think you can talk me out of my decision, Miss Vincent."

Suddenly Nellie spoke up.

"Vi," she said, "I'll be happy to take Clara's place at the lunch counter."

My mouth dropped open, but before I could say anything to the girl I had thought of as a friend, Vi came to my rescue.

"Mr. Phillips," she said, "if you fire this girl, I'm quitting, too."

It was his turn to look stunned. "You can't . . ."

"I most certainly can," Vi assured him.

Mr. Phillips started to say something, but Vi interrupted him.

She said, "You know that I have a standing invitation from the manager at El Tovar to transfer there."

"What about your mother? You can't leave her at the sanitarium here and run off to the Grand Canyon."

"Mother will understand. She's getting good care now and improving daily."

"We are short-handed already. If you leave, how will I keep the dining room going?"

"Let me point out, Mr. Phillips, that we are short-handed because you are too quick to fire the new girls Kansas City sends out. And when one lasts long enough for me to train, she immediately transfers to another Harvey House where the manager doesn't fire her once a day."

After Vi said that, Mr. Phillips hung his head so low his goatee touched his bow tie. But he recovered fast, and I wondered if Vi standing up to him was also a daily occurrence.

Immediately, he announced in his bossy tone that he would give me a chance. He put me on probation and told me I'd have to learn the Harvey way *overnight* or he'd send me packing, no matter how short-handed they got.

He couldn't put Nellie on probation right then, too, because she high-tailed it to our room. So he walked over and spoke to one of the chefs about not cutting the ham too thin.

"Thank you," I said to Vi. "You wait and see. I'll be the best Harvey Girl ever assigned to the Belen Harvey House."

She sighed. "Just prove I haven't made a mistake by putting my job on the line for a girl as green as the hills she left behind."

12

On-the-Job Training

"Turn out the light," Nellie demanded. "How do you expect me to get any sleep?"

"Sorry, I'm trying to hurry," I apologized, even though I knew it wasn't the light that woke her.

Another freight train had roared past the Harvey House, the fourth one so far that night. Every one caused the windowpanes to rattle, the floor to tremble, the bed springs and metal frames on both our beds to shake, and me to prick my finger with the sewing needle.

Nellie rolled over and returned to snoring.

It was two a.m. I was exhausted and wanted to be asleep, too. Instead, I was sitting on the edge of my bed with my borrowed uniform draped over my lap. My back was aching, and I knew it would take me another hour to finish altering the hem.

I was a slow seamstress, not having inherited the skills of my Grandma Massie. I hadn't wanted to drop the hem. That was Vi's idea. There was only enough material to drop it two inches, too little to meet Harvey standards. But I was determined to follow orders and once I started, I had to keep going. I couldn't wear a half-hemmed dress on the first full day of my life as a Harvey Girl.

While I hemmed, I tried to remember all the rules Vi had gone over with us. Then I memorized the cup code, which was the reason the Harvey Girls in all those dining rooms from Kansas City to New Mexico knew what drink a customer had ordered from another waitress.

One Harvey Girl took drink orders from customers and arranged their cups and saucers according to the code. For a coffee order, she put the cup upright in the saucer. For hot tea, upside down in the saucer. For iced tea, upside down and tilted against the saucer; for milk, upside down away from the saucer. A few minutes later, another Harvey Girl, called the drink girl, "deciphered" the code and served the drinks.

At ten 'til three, I finished hemming with barely an inch of thread to spare. Then I tried to smooth out the puckers, embarrassing proof of my lack of sewing skill. I sucked on my sore, pin-cushion finger, the one that had gotten in the way of the needle so many times. Finally, I turned out the light.

The next morning I felt more tired than if I'd never gone to bed. Before six a.m., Nellie and I and the other girls were downstairs eating breakfast in the small staff dining room near the kitchen, dressed in our proper uniforms. Well, theirs were proper.

I took tiny bites of oatmeal and did my best to swallow. I could barely keep my eyelids open. Even the aroma of scrambled eggs and country-cured ham couldn't wake me up.

Vi bustled into the dining room and gave us our schedules for the week.

"You'll work three shifts a day because we're so short-handed. The breakfast train arrives at six thirty sharp. Let's get a move on, girls."

Vi talked almost as fast as she moved.

"Nellie," she said, "you report to Mr. Phillips in the dining room. You'll be drink girl at the station he assigns you. Have you memorized the code?"

Nellie's answer surprised me. "Vi, to tell the truth," she said, "I'm having trouble learning the code. But Clara knows it already. I heard her practicing it all night. So I am sure she agrees it would be a good idea for you to assign her to the dining room and me to the lunchroom, since I wouldn't need to know the cup code serving at the counter."

I was flabbergasted that Nellie had the nerve to ask Vi if she could work the counter again.

"Clara needs to work the counter so she can hide her short uniform from Mr. Phillips," Vi said. "And if you need to hide from him, too, because you haven't memorized the cup code, then I'll assign you to clear away the dirty dishes after a customer finishes eating. We are short of busboys."

Nellie's expression showed her distaste for that task. "I'll manage just fine as a drink girl," she declared.

Vi said, "Now come with me. I'll teach you how to make the coffee."

When I stood up to follow, she saw my hem. "Good thing Fred Harvey's not paying you to make his uniforms." Then she told me I could use the iron in the basement, after the breakfast shift, to press my puckered hem.

In the lunchroom, Vi ushered me over to the gleaming, silver coffee urn. "This is your first duty every morning," she said. "And you must make a fresh pot every two hours, even if there's still some left. Throw out any that hasn't been served by then because it will taste boiled."

She showed me how to measure coffee grounds into the big urn and fill it with good-tasting water that didn't have an alkali taste. It came out of barrels shipped in from the Midwest.

While I was listening to her, I also heard the clang of the brass gong outside. That was the signal that the breakfast train was chugging up the tracks. Any second, it would stop out front and hungry passengers would disembark. My heart pounded.

"Follow the recipe precisely," Vi was saying. It was hard to hear over the sound of the locomotive. "Fred Harvey coffee has to taste exactly the same in Barstow, California, Amarillo or Slaton, Texas, or in any other Harvey House. Harvey standards must be maintained."

"To heck with Harvey standards," said a railroad man who burst into the lunchroom at the front of a mob of people when the cashier unlocked the door. "Worry about the *hombre* who's going to drink it before he makes a run to El Paso."

"Morning, Floyd," Vi said. "Meet Clara. She'll be working this station starting today."

Floyd tipped his fireman's cap and sat down on a stool on the other side of the marble counter from me. More railroad men quickly filled up five of the swivel stools on each side of him.

I stared at Floyd, my first customer. I knew what I was supposed to do. I followed the rule about standing away from the counter six inches and reminded myself to say "yes, sir" and "no, sir."

I opened my mouth, hoping for the best. "Uh, may I . . . I . . . I take your or . . . order, sir?"

Instead of sounding poised like the Harvey Girls I'd watched on the trip west, I sounded befuddled.

"Sure, Miss." Floyd grinned and looked at the other railroad men. When he had their attention, he rattled off his order.

"Bring me a plate of sinkers, a couple slabs of pork belly, and a cup of that java Mr. Harvey is so famous for. But hold the moo juice. I swore off moo juice when I got out of diapers."

"Sinkers? Java? Uh . . . uh . . . diapers?" I stammered.

One of the men a couple of stools away chortled. The expressions of the others were carbon copies of Floyd's grin.

"Go easy, boys," Vi said. "She's green as grass, and I need all the girls I can train."

To me she said, "They're harmless."

But that was all the help she gave me. She was through the swinging door into the kitchen without a hint of what I was to bring to my first customer.

I looked over at Hazel, who was serving at the other end of the counter. But she was busy with her own customers, not railroad men but bleary-eyed, half-asleep passengers.

Sinkers? I repeated to myself. It sounded familiar. Had I seen it on one of the menus in another Harvey House? No. Someone on one of the trains had mentioned sinkers. Then I knew. That Mrs. Wilder I sat next to on the train to Kansas City. She had told how the biscuits served in the early lunch hash houses along the railway were so heavy customers called them sinkers.

What was *pork belly?* Bacon, maybe. *Moo juice?* That could be milk or cream. *Java?* Java sounded like something I'd studied in one of Miss Forester's geography lessons. No, Floyd said it was something Fred Harvey was famous for. Suddenly I knew.

"Yes, sir," I said, confidence building with each word. "A plate of biscuits and bacon. And no cream with your java. With your coffee, that is. Right, sir?"

Floyd whistled, and the other men cheered and clapped.

And I was pleased with myself.

When the coffee was ready, I turned to the men and asked, "Do you'uns want coffee?"

The grins reappeared, but they nodded.

While I served the coffee, one man asked, "Where are you from, honey?"

"Missoura," I said.

Then he mimicked the way I'd pronounced it.

"Missour-uh, is it? And not Missour-e-e-e?"

Remembering the rule to "serve, not converse," I moved on down the counter, pouring coffee, and didn't answer.

Most of the men wanted fried eggs and ham. Two ordered French toast, sausage, and extra syrup. I stayed busy bringing in their orders four at a time from the kitchen.

I was slower than I wanted to be, and it was partly their fault because they kept asking questions.

"What do they feed 'Missoura' girls to grow them as tall as you?"

"Did you tie your mule up outside the kitchen door?"

"Is one of your legs shorter than the other from walking around those Ozark hills?"

Every question got a bigger laugh than the previous one from the men nearest Floyd, and my cheeks heated up 'til I felt them flaming.

I was as polite as I could be to them, but they kept it up.

Then one of the young ones, a telegrapher, judging by the carbon stains on his fingers, asked if I was making history as the first Ozark hillbilly to become a Harvey Girl.

The words left my mouth before I could stop them. "It's not nice to call somebody a hillbilly."

The men at the far end of the counter had been talking to each other about work. But they stopped when I spoke out and looked straight at me with serious looks on their faces.

"Dale's got bad manners, honey, but he didn't mean no harm by that remark," Floyd said. "He was teasing you."

"There's better ways to tease," I said, still feeling the hurt of the insult.

But deep down, I worried I'd been too quick to come to my own defense. Would I ever learn to be a polite Harvey Girl?

13

Butter Knives and Carrots Vichy

I could hear the toot-toot of the whistle, which meant the train was a mile down the track. I took a deep breath and slowly exhaled. The rush was about to begin. After two weeks of training, Vi had assigned me a new station for the evening shift. I still worked the lunch counter for breakfast and lunch, but after my properly fitting uniforms arrived, she also wanted me to wait on two tables in the dining room, sixteen customers at once.

The lunchroom of the Belen Harvey House was nice, but the dining room was high class. An hour before, I had spread out Irish linen tablecloths, folded starched napkins so they stood up like teepees at each place, and set my tables.

There was a lot of silverware. On the left of the dinner plate, I placed a salad fork and a dinner fork. The salad fork was the small one, and it was *only* used to eat the salad. On the right of the plate, I put the dinner knife. The blade had to face toward the plate. Next to it was a round spoon used for eating soup. Then came the short spoon for stirring coffee or eating a dessert, like custard.

A bent knife lay above the dinner plate. The first time Vi showed me one, I asked her what it was for. She explained it was used to spread butter, and it was considered bad manners to use any other knife for that purpose. Vi said that was the Harvey way.

A few minutes before the train arrived, Mr. Phillips and the cashier walked to the door. They got ready to greet the guests and offer a jacket to any man who arrived inappropriately attired. Harvey rules even extended to the passengers; men must wear jackets in the dining room.

Around the room stood Hazel, Nellie, Lizzie, Maude, Anna, and Virginia, the other Harvey Girls assigned to that shift with me.

Maude paced back and forth, and Anna peered through the lace curtains and watched the train as it pulled up. They looked confident, but my hands trembled a bit, matching the slight tremor that shook the hardwood floor. I checked my tables again. Perfect! When I heard the brass gong sound on the platform, my pulse raced. Then the gong was nearly drowned out by the roar of the engine, stopping a few yards from the dining room door.

At that moment, Vi scurried through the swinging doors from the kitchen and made a beeline to me.

"Did you place the silverware exactly one inch from the table's edge?" she shouted, inspecting my tables while she hopped around first one, then the other in a figure eight.

"Yes, Vi," I said, nodding in case she couldn't hear.

She moved one of the forks, though it didn't need straightening, and demanded, "Did you chill the salad plates?

"Yes, Vi." I bit my tongue.

"Did you add fresh ice to the water carafes?"

"Yes, Vi."

"Are the handles of the cups toward the customers?"

"Yes, ma'am!"

I wished I could answer, *I know my job!*

Vi was a bossy boss. Every day since I'd been in training, she made me do things over and over until they suited her—and Fred Harvey, too. She claimed he would turn over in his grave if he saw how some girls served. I tried to please her, even when I thought she was being persnickety.

As my first dining room passengers rushed in that night, I headed to the kitchen to pick up a tray loaded with salads. When I returned, the passengers were seated. I served the salads to one table and went back for the rest. By the time I'd served those, I could begin clearing away the empty salad plates at the first table, take them to the kitchen, and clear the others.

Next Mr. Phillips carried in the big tray of meat—roast beef, turkey, and ham—and I served the entree, as I'd learned to call the main course. Then I brought in the side dishes—bowls of white asparagus, carrots vichy, and red beets. While the customers ate, I made trip after trip to bring second helpings. After that course, I removed the dinner plates and served dessert.

As the passengers reboarded the train, I sighed in relief. I'd made it through my first dining room shift without a mistake. Vi never once corrected me although she had watched every move I made from the back of the room.

My final chore was to help the busboys clear the tables because we were once again short-handed. Mr. Phillips had fired a busboy that morning after a wet glass slipped out of his hand and shattered. I didn't mind cleaning up, since I knew my tips lay under the empty dessert plates.

As soon as Mr. Phillips headed for the kitchen, Estevan Chavez sneaked into the dining room. Estevan was the dark-skinned boy who had introduced himself as a call boy the day we arrived in Belen. I'd heard since then he wasn't really a call boy. In fact, that job was held by a grown man.

I thought Estevan was delivering a message. Anna and Lizzie glanced at him expectantly. Both often received notes from special *hombres*. But Estevan came to my station.

"*Buenas noches, señorita*," he said politely.

"Good evening to you, too," I answered, the same as I'd heard other girls respond to his greeting.

I was busy scraping off sticky crumbs from the dessert plates. So far I'd stacked six plates onto a tray and uncovered four dimes and three quarter tips, which I tucked into my pocket.

"That is a dirty chore. Such a dirty chore should be done by one, like myself, who does not wear a spotless uniform."

I glanced at my white pinafore. I had gotten through the shift without spilling anything.

"We are short-handed," I told Estevan. "You should apply for the job of busboy."

"It would be a pleasure to work for you, *señorita*," he said.

Apparently, he took my words to mean he was hired because he went right over to my other table and began clearing away dishes.

While I pondered how to explain that helping me probably was against the rules, he said, "Someday you will be a fine manager, like the nice *señora* who left before *Señor* Phillips came."

I had heard that the previous manager had transferred up the line to a larger Harvey House, one that was both a hotel and a dining room. It must have been a promotion. Then I smiled at the thought of me ever being the manager of a Harvey House. Not many women were.

"Now that truly would be getting above my raisin'," I said with a laugh.

Estevan laughed, but I could tell he didn't understand.

He cleared the table quickly. I suspected he often helped other girls in the dining room. While he worked, he kept one eye on the kitchen door. It was a good thing, too, because Mr. Phillips came back into the dining room to talk with the cashier.

Estevan disappeared. I finished up my work alone, aware that several of my tips and two forks at the second table were missing. Perhaps not all the customers had left tips, I consoled myself, and perhaps Estevan put the forks on another girl's tray.

I would have given Estevan two dimes for the work he did. One of the girls had told me he was the oldest of five children. His father had been killed in an accident while working on the railroad less than a month before I arrived. His mother, with child again, cleaned rooms in one of the boarding houses where the crews stayed. I had seen his younger brothers and sisters walking along the tracks, picking up lumps of coal that fell off the trains. Vi said they carried it home to heat their rundown adobe house.

Estevan's tips for delivering messages helped buy food for his family. So I didn't begrudge him the money, if he had taken my tips, but I wished he had waited for me to pay him. And I hoped those two forks would turn up in the kitchen.

14

A Fork in the Road

Waitressing was hard work. Sometimes my arms ached so much I could barely lift another tray of meals and balance it on the palm of my hand. My back and legs ached, too, and my feet stayed sore. The blisters those too-tight shoes rubbed on my heels burst and burned like fire. After I saved up, I bought new shoes at the Belen mercantile. Made of soft black leather, they were the finest I'd ever had.

Vi never let up on me. I had to prove myself a dozen times every shift. When I did things right, she was stingy with a compliment. When I made a mistake, she was quick to correct me, especially the first time Nellie got us into trouble by breaking the Harvey rules.

Nellie sweet-talked two of the best-looking chefs—Gregory from Germany and Victor from Italy—into teaching us to pronounce the names of the elegant dishes on the dinner menu.

Imagine me with my Ozark accent asking the customers, "Would you care for the Medaillon of Salmon Poche in Sauce Mousseline?"

Truth to tell, though, my accent didn't draw attention to itself. People from all over the world with accents of their own ate Fred Harvey meals. Railroad men came from every state. Indians from reservations, who spoke their Native American tongues, sold pottery and jewelry to the passengers. Mexicans farmed or worked other jobs around Belen. And Harvey Girls came from everywhere—the Mid-west, other parts of the U.S., and even from Europe.

The customers I served couldn't say "artichokes a la Grecque" any better than I could. Still, I watched what I said, erasing the most embarrassing Ozark words from my speech. I especially tried to keep "you'uns" from slipping out, although I couldn't see why it was any different than Southerners saying, "y'all" or Northerners saying, "youse."

I was grateful for those lessons from the chefs. It took practice to learn those foreign words, and to make matters worse, the menus changed every four days. Meals by Fred Harvey meant the highest quality of food but also that a passenger traveling from the West Coast to the Midwest would not have to eat the same thing twice on the trip.

One evening after a new menu arrived, Gregory, Victor, Nellie, and I sat on a bench in the park beside the Harvey House, practicing our pronunciation. I inhaled the fresh fall scent, a pleasant change after breathing the stifling air of the hot kitchen all day.

A few minutes later, Vi caught us. She came up behind me just as Nellie pinched her nose and said, "Fresh Shrimp with Noodles *all rotten*" instead of *au gratin*. We all burst out laughing.

"It's a good thing I'm the one that caught you. Mr. Phillips would have fired you for breaking the Harvey rule against employees dating."

"But, Vi," Nellie said, "we are working, going over the new menu. Fred Harvey would be proud."

"Mr. Phillips would not," Vi said.

Neither of the chefs had much to say in English. And I didn't understand what they said in their own languages.

Vi warned us, "Don't break this rule again, or I'll have to tell Mr. Phillips. In fact, don't break any of the Harvey rules. That includes the curfew."

I said, "Good night," and ran into the dormitory.

Then I spent a sleepless night, planning not to let Nellie get me into trouble again.

The next day was our day off. Days off came around once a week, and it would have felt good to sleep in. But Nellie wanted to see the sights.

What she meant by "sights" were tall, muscular, and eligible. That day the "sight" she was seeing was Randy Brady, a bow-legged ranch hand outfitted in a dusty sheepskin coat, even dustier cowboy boots and hat, and a big grin that showed his tobacco-stained teeth. He worked on a cattle ranch west of Belen and came into the Harvey House when his boss sent him to town for supplies. That's how Nellie met him. He was a friendly sort and tipped handsomely.

When he pulled up to the back of the Harvey House, he left his automobile running and stepped out to greet Nellie. His cheek bulged with a chaw of tobacco, and he spit the juice onto the ground.

His topless auto sputtered and coughed and rattled and choked, and twice he jumped back in to rev it up. I had my doubts about getting into the backseat with Hazel and May, the other girls Nellie invited. I held back as blonde-haired May climbed in.

Hazel nudged me toward the motorcar with her red fingernails, which she had polished to match her lipstick. She looked right pretty. It wasn't against the rules to paint your nails and lips on your day off. The three of us, all bundled in warm overcoats, squeezed in along with a picnic basket of leftovers, two bottles of water, and Randy's tool kit. I'd borrowed my coat from Anna, a girl from Colorado.

As we got to the steel bridge over the Rio Grande, I asked, "Isn't it too late in the fall for a picnic?"

Nellie, in the front beside Randy, shouted over her shoulder, "The food is just in case. . . . "

"Just in case of what?" I shouted back.

She faced the front and left me pondering.

In case this dilapidated auto breaks down in the desert? In case we don't get back by the curfew?

Hazel patted me on the hand and asked, "Where's your sense of adventure?"

After we crossed the river and headed south over several bumpy irrigation culverts, I tried to relax and enjoy the scenery. I watched the sun rise over the Manzano Mountains and wondered if this "adventure" would cost me my job.

For the first couple of hours, I tried to keep track of where we were "just in case" we had to trudge back on foot. But I gave up after we passed six windmills, drove through five dry gullies (May called them *arroyos*), bounced back and forth across the railroad tracks countless times, and came to so many forks in the road that I couldn't remember where we took the left and where the right.

The only fork in the road that I'd never forget was an actual three-pronged fork. About six feet tall, it was carved out of wood and stuck into the ground where two dirt roads came together. On it was a sign that announced it was—A Fork in the Road. May said she hoped someday to serve a customer big enough to use it. Nellie pondered what size tip he'd leave. And we all giggled.

Hazel jabbered away about her young man, whose name was Wayne Montgomery. Wayne was going to make the perfect husband. He had no faults, unless you counted his shyness. He had not yet proposed.

About mid-afternoon after traveling up, down, and around several narrow, crooked roads, we arrived in Magdelena.

"We have three miles to go," Randy shouted over his shoulder.

Nellie, May, Hazel, and I looked the town over. It was a railhead.

"This town is the whoop-it-up trail's end," May explained, "for cattle drives out of Arizona. It's a great place to meet people."

She meant eligible men.

Hazel added, "Don't forget about the mines around here."

More men, I assumed, some of whom might have struck it rich.

I saw a mercantile, two banks, and three other establishments that looked like saloons. There were churches, too, and a school, a cafe, and a gas station. Hazel pointed out cattle, waiting in nearby stockyards for shipment by rail. That accounted for the odor in the town.

When we finally stopped, we were out in the desert again at the campsite of a big cattle drive. Since the stockyards in Magdelena were already full, these cattle had to wait their turn outside of town. And they had to be tended to by the cowboys who had driven them across the state.

The cowboys were the cause of our all-day excursion. The fun began as soon as Randy helped us out of the car. And it was fun, even for me, the only one of us not shopping for a husband. The cowboys were plenty friendly. May, with her blonde hair, and Hazel, with her painted lips, got a lot of attention. Nellie would have gotten more, but Randy stuck right close. One of the tallest fellows chatted a while with me, too. We traded stories about where we were raised and how we came to be out West.

Welcoming the cattle drives was a favorite pastime for lots of folks from surrounding towns. Joining right in with the ones already there, we followed our noses to the chuck wagon and lined up. The "grub," as the cook called it, was spicy beans flavored with onions, barbecue sauce, hot peppers that burned my mouth, and a hunk of stringy meat. A tin cup of boiled coffee and two gritty biscuits completed the Meal-NOT-by-Fred-Harvey.

After we ate, we sat around a campfire and sang along with the cowboys. I didn't know the words to the Western songs, but I added my alto when they sang "America the Beautiful" and some of the sacred old hymns.

I was sorry when Randy claimed it was time to head back to Belen. He had no trouble rounding up Nellie, May, and me. But finding Hazel took us the better part of an hour. She had gone for a walk. When Hazel and a cowboy I didn't recognize sauntered back toward the campfire hand in hand, Randy approached them.

"Hazel, let's go," Randy said.

"Who are you to tell Hazel what to do?" demanded the cowboy.

"I'm the one who brought her here," Randy told him.

The cowboy planted his boots in the sand. "Well, I'm the one she came to see!"

"I'm the one who's taking her back to Belen," Randy said, spitting tobacco juice on the ground. "And I don't have time to argue. Hazel, are you coming?"

"Of course, Randy," she said, letting go of the cowboy's hand. "I'm sorry, Wayne. I have to go now."

So this was Wayne. He didn't appear the least bit shy to me. I stared along with Hazel, Randy, Nellie, May, and ten or twelve others who had gathered around as he dropped to his knees, removed his sweaty cowboy hat, grabbed Hazel's hand, and proposed marriage.

She said, "Yes!" and we applauded. There were congratulatory hugs and handshakes plus explanations of who Randy was and why he was taking Hazel back to the Harvey House. Then we dashed off to Randy's auto. If Wayne felt embarrassed, he didn't show it while he helped Hazel get situated in the backseat. As we drove off, he was telling Hazel he'd buy an engagement ring with his cattle drive money and deliver it the next weekend.

"There's nothing like a dollop of jealousy," May said, when we were a mile or two down the road, "to bring a man to his knees."

The trip back was almost without mishap. Randy drove faster than I thought possible on those sandy roads. Until we were within a mile of the Harvey House, I was sure we would get back before the curfew.

It was Nellie's fault that we didn't. Not long after we crossed the steel bridge over the river, our headlights shone on the eyes of a big jackrabbit in the road. It froze.

"Watch out!" Nellie shouted, grabbing Randy's arm and causing the auto to swerve into the sharp edge of an irrigation culvert.

Unharmed, the jackrabbit hopped off into the brush when the lights went out. The left front tire, however, hissed flat.

"We're stranded," Nellie said as we climbed out of the car.

I countered, "We can walk from here."

"Walk!" Nellie, May, and Hazel yelled. "We'll do no such thing!"

Randy was already lifting the spare out of the back while I pondered what to do. Walk, and make it back before Vi closed up for the night. Or wait, and be late for sure.

I walked. Alone. In the dark. With that borrowed coat buttoned up tight. But I could see the lights of the Harvey House the whole way. My heart was pounding and my hands shook as I opened the door to the dormitory and went in. The light in the entry was still on. No one was around, but I could hear Vi at the top of the stairs, talking to someone. I couldn't see her. I hoped that meant she couldn't see me. Nor could I make out everything she said. I caught a few words. The last was "good night." Then I knew she was headed down to lock up.

I slipped into the kitchen, shut the door behind me, and hoped she wouldn't hear my loud panting. It only took her a few minutes to come down the creaky stairs, lock the outside door, go back up, and turn out the light.

I stood on tiptoes at the high window in the employees' dining room and peeked out. I heard the familiar rattle of the dilapidated auto. Randy was driving with the headlights off, but when he stopped under a street lamp, I glimpsed three figures climb out and race across the park.

I met them at the back door. They tiptoed in, making more noise than necessary. I relocked the door and herded them toward the kitchen.

No one spoke until we were standing by the sink. They wasted time thanking me. I shushed them and told them if we didn't get past Vi's room without her seeing us, she would suspect we had come in after the curfew.

We were quiet for several minutes. Then Nellie came up with a plan. One by one, ten minutes apart, we would sneak up to our rooms. It worked for everyone, but me. Maybe it was because I was last. Maybe it was because I had the biggest feet and made the loudest noise on the stairs. Vi caught me at the top of the stairs.

She opened door to her room and barked, "You're late!"

I started, but I answered truthfully, "I wasn't late, Vi. I came in before the curfew."

She pointed to the overcoat over my arm. "Why are you coming up the stairs, carrying that?"

"I'm returning it to Anna." That was the truth, too.

Vi knit her brows.

I continued walking toward my room.

She couldn't fire me. There was no Harvey rule against carrying a borrowed overcoat down the hall after the curfew.

15

Under Suspicion

After two months on the job, my life was good. But it would have been better if Nellie hadn't pestered me daily.

"Vi won't even have to know," she said.

"How do you figure that?" I asked.

"We could switch stations once a week on the days Vi goes to visit her mother." Vi's mother was a lunger, a patient at a sanitarium in Albuquerque.

"Someone will tattle," I assured her.

"I'll split my tips for that day with Hazel," Nellie said. "She won't tell."

"I don't want to get into trouble," I said, making my answer sound final.

A few days later, she asked Mr. Phillips to switch us.

"A hard-working manager doesn't have time to deal with such trivial matters," he said.

So finally Nellie came right out and asked Vi.

"Vi," she said, "if you trained me to work the lunch counter, I could fill in if something happens to Clara."

She's fibbing, I thought. *The real reason is she wants to meet eligible railroad men because things didn't work out between her and Randy Brady.* I was tempted to talk to Vi myself when Nellie wasn't around. Then I remembered the fib I'd told. And Nellie knew my secret. I couldn't tell Vi the truth.

Thank goodness, Vi's answer was, "I don't see any reason to switch you girls."

I was relieved. I didn't want to change. I was getting along fine working the lunch counter for two shifts each day. The breakfast crew didn't tease me after the first day when the telegrapher called me a hillbilly. I felt sorry I'd been blunt because the men seemed to think I couldn't take a joke.

But the lunch crew knew better. Those "rails" were a jovial lot. Some dressed in overalls, striped denim caps, and red or blue bandanas round their necks. Conductors and porters wore blue serge uniforms. In our Harvey House, the black porters ate right at the counter. In some houses, I'd heard, they had to eat in a special dining room in the back and be served by busboys. All of them from engineers to firemen to flagmen loved to pull pranks on the Harvey staff.

They tracked in mud so that the busboys had "plenty to keep them busy." They hid the salt and pepper shakers, then claimed I'd never put them out. They pulled horny toads out of their pockets to surprise me. When I screamed, they cautioned, "Not so loud, Clara. You're scaring the poor critter."

But most of all, they liked to tease Mr. Phillips. They thought he was a sissy. On their way back to the trains after eating, they loudly threatened to report him to the Fred Harvey bigwigs because the ham was sliced too thin.

"The story goes," one of the engineers told me, "that Fred Harvey's dying words were, 'Don't cut the ham too thin.'"

Mr. Phillips took that and every other legend about Fred Harvey to heart. His personal mission was to carry on the Harvey tradition.

Mr. Phillips spent most of his time in the dining room and left the lunch counter to manage on its own. Truth to tell, I knew Nellie would like the relaxed feeling at the lunch counter. She would especially love meeting the men. The crews paid with coupons from the rail company, but they tipped generously if a girl went along with their pranks. If they were sweet on a girl, Hazel told me, they tipped with turquoise or silver jewelry they bought from the Indians out front. One time Hazel showed me all the pretty pieces she'd collected when she worked my end of the counter. She let me pick out a bracelet for Alice.

My tip earnings were piling up, but, much to my relief, I never got a piece of Indian jewelry. I liked the railroad men, but I didn't encourage their flirtations. And I had a sneaking suspicion that Vi knew that. When I was on the job, I was all business—unless I saw a horny toad.

All that came to a halt, though, when Hazel quit to marry Wayne Montgomery, and Vi assigned Nellie to take her place.

The day she started at the counter Nellie made one mistake after another. Watching her, you'd think she was a brand-new Harvey Girl.

As she backed through the swinging doors from the kitchen, carrying a tray full of orders, she got turned around. Instead of heading over to serve her customers, she walked right over to mine. Balancing the tray on one hand, she used her other hand to set a plate of ham and eggs in front of Alkali Jack, the cutest, most eligible engineer on the Horny Toad.

He grinned real big before he winked at the other guys and asked her, "Is this your first day on the job, Red Riding Hood?"

Nellie smiled sweetly and nodded.

"Jack ordered hotcakes," said the fireman on his left. "He likes his sweets hot, Miss Copper Penny."

All the men hooted, and Nellie got flustered and acted shy. I'd never known her to be shy before. But I went to her rescue. I took the plate and put it back on the tray.

"Your station is over there," I said, pointing toward the other end of the room.

She didn't thank me.

As she headed over to serve her customers, another of the men asked, "Jack, do you like carrot cake as much as you like hotcakes?"

That got another laugh. And Nellie, who usually looked annoyed when anyone called her Carrot Top, glanced at Alkali Jack. I didn't hear what he said because my orders were up in the kitchen. When I came back, I did hear several of her customers complain she'd mixed up their orders.

After she straightened them out, I thought things had settled into the usual routine, until I came out of the kitchen and found her clearing away my customers' empty plates and dirty silverware.

"Lost again?" I asked in a none-too-friendly tone.

"You looked like you needed help," she said.

That really aggravated me.

Two of Nellie's customers started clamoring for service. I wanted to tell her she was the one needing help, but I was younger than she was, not dumber. The game she was playing was clear. She hoped I'd wait on her customers while she flirted with the railroad men.

I didn't budge from my station. I kept right on doing my work, even though she stepped on my toes twice. I gathered up the rest of the dirty plates, stacked them on a tray, and hefted it up on one hand. I planned to carry it to the kitchen, but Nellie blocked my path. When I took a step, I stumbled into her, jostling the tray and rattling the dishes. It took me several seconds to balance it again.

Meanwhile, the eyes of all the men at the counter were on Nellie. She was apologizing all over herself in a voice I'd always imagined Mary Pickford would use in a love scene with Douglas Fairbanks—if you could hear movie stars talk on the screen.

"Here, let me help you," she said. "It's my fault. Really it is."

She grabbed the tray to steady it, but because she was shorter than me, it tipped toward her. Dishes, glasses, silverware, and food scraps slid onto the floor. The clatter could be heard above the laughter, but not above my scream.

"You clumsy, stupid girl!" I shouted. "Look what you made me do!"

"Sorry," she whispered.

And I immediately knew I would be blamed—for my outburst. I had acted like my dad, calling somebody clumsy and stupid. I felt ashamed. I felt the blood rising to my cheeks. I swallowed hard to get my temper under control. My job could be at stake when Vi got back from visiting her mother. The Harvey way did not include yelling at another Harvey Girl, especially in front of the customers.

My anger cooled when I looked at the mess. The floor wasn't the worst of it. Besides, the two new busboys would clean that. Nellie's pinafore had been splattered with egg yolk, ham grease, and blueberry jelly. The laundry would never get the stains out.

"You'll have to change," I said. "Go on. I'll cover for you here."

She headed upstairs so fast she forgot to lay down the handful of silverware she had been clearing away.

The next day when Vi came back from visiting her mother, I stayed extra busy to avoid her. But it didn't keep me out of trouble. Someone had tattled on me. Vi made that clear the minute she sat me down in the manager's office.

She paced back and forth when she started in on me. "I have been told," she said, "that yesterday you acted in a manner unbecoming a well-trained Harvey Girl."

I didn't ask who had tattled, and Vi didn't reveal her name.

First, she reminded me that a Harvey Girl must always exhibit good manners in front of the customers. Then she said, "Clara, I am going to assign you to the dining room. Permanently. From now on Nellie will take your station at the lunch counter."

It was a good thing she dismissed me then because I was steaming. And the person I was angriest with was Nellie. She had managed to get exactly what she wanted. She would be serving the railroad men, and I would be in the dining room every shift, serving passengers under the critical eyes of Vi *and* Mr. Phillips.

I stomped up to our room in an un-Harvey-Girl-like fashion. When I opened the door, Nellie was there. She was in her uniform, kneeling on the floor beside an open trunk I'd never seen before. The second she saw me she dropped something into the trunk and slammed the lid down with a bang.

"Oh my goodness," she said, putting her hand to her throat, "you gave me a start."

I took a couple of deep breaths. I wanted to lash out at her, but I couldn't risk another scolding from Vi. *A Harvey Girl uses good manners at all times*, I kept thinking. I stomped over, plopped down on my bed, and ignored her.

"Did you see what Hazel gave me before she left?" Nellie asked. She stood up and smoothed out her uniform.

Instead of answering, I picked up the postal card Nellie must have laid on my bed. It was from Alice. I had written to her in care of my teacher, Miss Forester, at the one-room school.

Alice had written in big block letters, "I mis you. Beulah is bad sick. Come home soon. Luv, Alice. Beulah sends her luv to."

A wave of homesickness washed over me. I stared out the window at the mountains to the east, the direction back to the Ozarks.

"Did you see it, Clara?" Nellie asked again, pointing to the trunk she had slammed shut.

When I still didn't answer, Nellie did the talking.

"It's a hope chest," she said. "I already have a few things to put in it, things I'll need when I find the right man to marry me."

She had told me lots of times she'd been buying pretty things for her trousseau. I never knew when she had the time since she dragged me with her on her days off, and we had only gone shopping once. Twice she promised to show me her things, but she was always too busy or tired or sleepy. She didn't offer to then, I suppose, because someone knocked on the door.

"Come in," she shouted.

Bertha, the heavyset kitchen girl who made salads, opened the door a crack and peeked in.

"Mr. Phillips wants everyone in the kitchen right away," she said. "He sent me to round up the staff for a meeting."

"Why?" Nellie asked.

Bertha shrugged. "All I know is somebody must have waved a red bandana in his face. He's acting like a bull, madder than I've ever seen him before."

I had the worst feeling that I was the cause of his anger. Was he going to override Vi's punishment and fire me?

In the kitchen, we lined up in three ragged rows—chefs, kitchen help, busboys, Harvey Girls—and waited. I stood at the back, like always.

Mr. Phillips hadn't come in yet, but Vi asked for everyone's attention, which she already had, and started the meeting.

"This is as good a time as any," she said, "to make an announcement."

Right then a scowling Mr. Phillips came through the swinging doors from the dining room. But he didn't interrupt.

"Two weeks from now a big dinner is scheduled at the Casteñada," Vi said.

We all knew what that meant. Some of our staff would have a chance to work at that famous Harvey House in Las Vegas, New Mexico, for a few days. The Casteñada, a much larger and grander house than ours, had been the site of the annual Rough Riders reunion ever since 1899 because many of the Rough Riders themselves had come from New Mexico. Every year there were parades, dances, and rodeos. Teddy Roosevelt himself had visited the Casteñada many times. So had lots of other famous people.

"The manager there has asked me to hand pick the staff I take with me," Vi continued. "I'll choose two chefs, one kitchen worker, and two Harvey Girls."

In the next few days, we would all be on our best behavior, competing for a chance to go with Vi. I wanted to go more than anything. Someone asked Vi who would be attending the dinner. It was a group of suffragists led by Carrie Chapman Catt. I could hardly believe my ears. She was one of the courageous women Miss Forester had told us scholars about. She was working to get the Nineteenth Amendment to the Constitution ratified so that women could vote. I thought how proud I'd be to see Carrie Chapman Catt in person and then write about it in letters to Miss Forester and to my sisters.

Mr. Phillips shooed Vi out of the way so he could talk. "A member of this staff is a thief," is what he said. "A common criminal who will be caught and punished. Every employee in this Harvey House is under suspicion. One of you is guilty. And when I find out who you are . . ." He paused and glared at us.

I tried not to fidget.

"When I find out who you are," he went on, "you will not only be fired and made to pay restitution for the things you have stolen from this Harvey House, you will be blacklisted. You will never, never be able to find employment in a Fred Harvey establishment again."

The lunch train pulled up out front, and Mr. Phillips ordered us back to work.

During that shift and the next, the rumors flew. I didn't know how much was true. I overheard the baker tell May that silverware, linens, and china had been taken. Then May told him that Mr. Phillips suspected customers at first. He reasoned that many of them wanted Fred Harvey souvenirs. But he watched them for several days and concluded it wasn't them because things went missing after the customers reboarded the trains.

"So," Bertha, the salad girl, told me, "Mr. Phillips decided it must be someone on the staff." She had gotten it all from the cashier, who had gotten it all straight from the horse's mouth, or so he claimed.

"Who does he think is guilty?" I asked.

But Bertha didn't know. She herself suspected Estevan, who was now a busboy.

I raised my eyebrows at that. Estevan? A sneak thief? I supposed it was possible. He was often underfoot. But . . .

Or, she hinted, it could be someone about to "go to housekeeping," someone who wanted to set a fancy table.

That hit me hard. I didn't know Hazel all that well, but she had always been nice. I didn't like thinking she had stolen things from Fred Harvey.

Then Bertha whispered that Mr. Phillips was watching all of us. My pulse speeded up.

16

Catching a Sneak Thief

Being under suspicion made me jittery. For days, I dropped things and forgot to finish what I was doing. The more I tried to do my best work, the more I did my worst. Yet I still hoped Vi would pick me to go to the Casteñada.

Toward the end of the next week, I was in the dining room setting my two tables before the dinner train arrived.

Vi was on the other side of the room, teaching a new girl how to place the silverware. Mr. Phillips was consulting with the cashier about a shipment of cigars and dime novels for the newsstand.

Wearing a perfectly fitted, spotless uniform, I felt like a fancy lady in a fancy room. The lights were dimmed, casting a soft glow over everything. Walnut wainscotting went all the way around the room. The decor was rich and elegant. The windows were covered in white lace, and above the door was a stained glass panel done in a green and yellow flower design. I finished up my tables, glanced over them one last time, and then waited for the train.

I gazed at the lithograph in a gilt frame hanging on the wall. It was the same Thomas Moran painting of the Grand Canyon that was on the postal card Granny 'hite had shown me. Every time I looked at it, I felt uplifted. It reminded me of my dream to travel. Of course, I'd traveled all the way from Missoura to New Mexico. But I wanted to travel again. I wanted to work at the Harvey House on the canyon's rim. And if Vi would pick me to go to the Casteñada, I'd have the experience of serving at an important dinner.

Someday . . . if . . .

"I am talking to you, Clara!" Mr. Phillips dragged my attention back from my dreams.

"I'm sorry, sir. Is something wrong?"

He pointed to one of the tables I had set. "Did you do this?"

"Yes, sir." I scanned the table. It looked fine to me.

"Did you check the crystal for chips?"

I tried to remember. "I think so, sir."

"Obviously, you did not!"

He picked up one of the stems and held up to the light. Then he shoved it so close to my nose I couldn't focus on it.

"Do you see the chip?"

All I saw were his smudged fingerprints on the glass, but I didn't argue.

"I'll replace it immediately, sir."

"You will reset the entire table," he said.

He grabbed the edge of the tablecloth and yanked it off the table. With it came the china, crystal, and silver. Eight place settings crashed into a heap at my feet.

I gasped. Mr. Phillips had done what Fred Harvey was said to have done when he inspected a table and found it lacking.

"Now start over," he ordered. "And this time do it right."

The whistle of the train tooted a mile down the track as I stooped to clear away the mess and put the table to rights.

I gritted my teeth. *A Harvey Girl always, always, always displays nice manners,* I thought. *Even when she has just ruined her chance to go to the Casteñada.* I knew that Vi had been watching from across the room.

When I went to bed that night, it took me a while to drift off. Two freight trains roared up the tracks, but I had gotten used to the ground rumbling and the windowpanes rattling when one sped past. What bothered me was the mistake I'd made. A tiny chip in one of the crystal stems. I should have been more careful. A skilled Harvey Girl would never have let that slip her notice. And now Vi would choose one of the other girls to go to the Casteñada. Someone else would have the privilege of waiting on Carrie Chapman Catt.

Apparently, Nellie could tell I was restless when I rolled over for the tenth time. She was kneeling on the floor, peering into her hope chest.

"I'll turn out the light if you want me to," she said.

"The light's not bothering me. My feet hurt."

Being on my feet all day made them ache constantly even though I had new shoes. Those shoes were the only purchase I'd made with the money I'd earned. I had the rest saved up in a stocking under my mattress. My monthly salary was in paper money, and my tips were in silver coin—dozens of dimes, fourteen quarters, and one half-dollar, left by a rich rancher. It was the most money I'd ever seen in one place, more money than my dad earned in three years selling the hogs he raised. I thought about putting it in a bank the way Vi had suggested to all the girls. But I liked having it near me, counting it, dreaming of the traveling I could do with it.

I worried some, after Mr. Phillips told us there was a thief among us. Who could it be? Estevan? Hazel? If it had been her, then I was safe because she had left. But what if it was someone else? Someone nearby. Someone I trusted. . . .

Nellie turned out the light and got into bed. I relaxed, pulled the covers up to my chin, and took a long deep breath. Several minutes went by. I'm not sure how many because I drifted off.

What caused my eyes to pop open was the clinking of silver. Had I been dreaming about setting my tables? No, there it was again, softer this time, a metallic ding.

I lay as still as I could, trying to see. The shades were drawn, and the room was dark. After a bit, though, I could make out a figure in a dress. It must be the thief. And she had my silver coins. Somehow she had pulled my stocking out from under the mattress with me sleeping on top of it. My money! I threw the covers off, sat up, and yanked the chain of the lamp on the night table.

I hollered, "I caught the thief!"

Then I blinked, twice. It was Nellie. She stood at the edge of her bed fully dressed in a dark frock. I reached under my mattress to feel my money stocking. It was still there.

I rubbed my eyes and tried to wake up enough to say I was sorry for calling her a thief. But she spoke first.

"Oh, Clara, don't tell on me. Please don't. I'm going to return it all."

I frowned and blinked and frowned again. Then I noticed the pile of things on her bed. Silverware, china, linens. And one glance at the Fred Harvey patterns told me they weren't things she had bought with her earnings.

She began to weep, silently, with her head bowed. Still sleepy, I tried to make sense of what I saw on the bed.

She wiped at her eyes and got herself under control.

"I know it was wrong," she said. "I don't know what I was thinking. At first, it was only a fork to keep as a souvenir. Then it was a teacup. And then . . ." She waved her hand across the things on the bed. "I got carried away."

What could I say?

"I'm going to return them now," she said, "because I . . . I . . . I'm not even engaged yet."

"What time is it?"

"A few minutes past midnight." She ran her hand through her mussed up hair.

I had been asleep quite a while.

"Will you help me?" she asked, blinking as fresh tears ran down her cheeks.

I shook my head. "I can't risk losing my job. You took them. You return them."

"I can't carry them all at once," she said. "But if you help, we can make one trip down to the kitchen, put them away, and no one would be the wiser."

The very thought of tiptoeing down the hall and down the creaky stairs so close to Vi's room and into the kitchen carrying stolen silver and china caused me to shake all over.

"No!" I said. "Don't ask me to risk my job."

"I'm not asking. I'm begging. Please."

"No!" I shook my head so fast I got dizzy.

"But you have to help me. You owe it to me." Her tears had stopped.

"Where did you get a fool notion like that?"

She narrowed those azure eyes to slits.

"I don't know what you're talking about, Nellie."

"I'm talking about your little secret," she said in a snippy voice.

If I didn't help her and she got fired, all she had to do was tell Vi how old I really was. And both of us would be on the breakfast train headed east.

I got dressed. She told me to wear dark clothing so we could stay hidden in the shadows. The only thing I had was my black Harvey Girl dress, so I put that on without a white pinafore, which made me feel half-dressed. I was disguising myself in half my uniform to return stolen goods. I didn't know which part made me feel more like a traitor to the Harvey Girl tradition.

Minutes later, I tiptoed down the dark hall behind Nellie, carrying six place settings of silverware wrapped tightly in Fred Harvey linen. My palms were sweating on the fine cloth.

I was aggravated at Nellie, of course, but the person I was never going to forgive was myself for confiding in her on the train.

The only light came from under the closed bathroom door. But it was enough for us to find our way. I listened at the door of each bedroom, wondering if anyone in the dormitory was still awake. At the top of the stairs, we paused at Vi's door. She wasn't snoring, like she sometimes did.

Nellie stayed close to the wall after she started down the stairs. Moonlight shining through the high window above the landing made it easier to see. Slowly, very slowly, she stepped down one step, waited, then stepped down on the next.

I stayed at the top of the stairs, barely two feet from Vi's door. The pounding of my heart would probably wake her.

When Nellie reached the landing, I started down. The wooden steps squeaked. I was sure Vi was going to throw open her door and catch me red-handed.

By the time I reached the landing, Nellie was on the first floor. I could hear a freight train approaching. I didn't move until it was rumbling past the building. Then I hurried down the rest of the stairs. The train's noise covered up the squeaks of the stairs.

Nellie was already in the kitchen with the light on, putting away the china when I got there. I opened the big drawer, unwrapped the silverware, laid it on the counter, and shoved the linens down the laundry chute to the basement.

"You shouldn't have done that," Nellie whispered. "Someone will notice in the morning."

"They're soiled," I said. "I sweated all over them."

I started putting the silverware into the drawer. My hands were shaking so much I dropped two forks on the floor. They clanked against each other, making a lot of racket in the big empty room.

I put the rest of the silver away, and then stooped to pick up the forks. What should I do with them? I couldn't put dirty forks in the drawer. Should I wash them? Or leave them in the sink? I didn't want to get the dishwasher into trouble. Mr. Phillips might fire him.

Nellie said, "Just put them in the drawer."

I couldn't. Customers expected everything to be clean when they ate at a Harvey House.

She grabbed one of the forks out of my hand and moved toward the drawer.

"You can't," I said. "Not without washing it."

"Don't be silly, Clara."

I stood firm and waved my fork at her. She waved hers back at me, like it was a short sword. We were fighting like that—clink, clink—when the kitchen door burst open and Vi scampered in, wearing a fluffy gray bathrobe.

I almost dropped my fork again. Nellie hid hers behind her back.

Vi stared at us.

If I could have found my voice, I know I would have made a clean breast of everything.

The awkward silence finally ended when Vi demanded, "What's going on here?"

Nellie whispered, "It's not what you think."

"You don't know what I'm thinking," Vi countered.

"Well, I can guess," Nellie said. "You think we are guilty, but we're not."

"You *are* guilty," Vi said. "Of something. Otherwise you wouldn't be downstairs in the middle of the night, dueling with forks."

Vi laughed at her own joke. I might have thought it comical, too, if I hadn't been about to lose my job.

"You've been watching too many Douglas Fairbanks movies," she said.

Nellie forced a laugh, but all I could manage was a nervous giggle.

Then Nellie said, "We were hungry. And Clara suggested we sneak down here and see if there was any of that lemon meringue pie left from dinner."

That, of course, was an outright lie. I detest meringue as much as blinky milk. But I managed to nod and tell a whopper of my own. "Robert's lemon meringue looks delicious."

Once you start telling fibs, does it become a habit?

Vi stared at us again, like she was making up her mind about how to punish us. Then she nodded, too.

"Yes, a piece of pie. Let's all have one," Vi said.

For me, that was a punishment.

Nellie handed her the dirty fork she was holding, got a clean one out of the drawer for herself, and went to the pantry for the pie. I set out plates and found a knife. Vi poured three glasses of milk. We carried our pie and milk to the staff dining room and sat down.

My hands were trembling, so I hid them under the table with my shaky knees while Vi and Nellie started in on their pies. Meringue. It made me gag to look at it. How could I force it down with a fork that had been on the floor? I gripped the edge of the chair seat with one hand and took a tiny bite. I swallowed fast. Then I drank some milk. My stomach churned.

Nibbling slowly, I had half a piece left when Vi and Nellie took their last bites. Vi laid down her fork. I laid mine down, too. Nellie eyed my plate, and I knew she was going to tell me to hurry and finish.

Instead, she asked, "If you don't want the rest of that, Clara, can I have it?"

"Sure," I said, shoving it over to her. "I guess I'm not as hungry as I thought. But that was the best meringue I've ever eaten."

Now that wasn't a lie. It was the best, but I still didn't like it.

I stretched my arms and yawned, thinking we could all go back to bed right after we washed the dishes.

But Vi wasn't ready to leave.

"I'm glad I caught you two girls tonight," she said.

Caught. My stomach churned, and I could feel meringue coming back up.

"I've had my eye on both of you," she said. "And I've made a decision."

Like any good waitress, Nellie stacked our dirty plates and forks. But I sensed she was doing it to busy her hands.

"I'm pleased with the work you two do," Vi said. "Nellie, you're doing an expert job at the lunch counter. It seems to suit you better than the dining room. And, Clara, I was especially pleased to see the manners you displayed after Mr. Phillips performed his Fred Harvey imitation with the tablecloth."

I realized I was holding my breath.

Vi went on, "So I'm taking the two of you to the Casteñada with me next week."

I allowed myself to breathe again.

17

The Well Country

The morning train to Albuquerque was due. Vi, Nellie, and I waited for it trackside under the portal of our Harvey House.

"Look at these," Nellie said, admiring the handmade pottery and jewelry laid out on the blankets of the Isleta Indians. "Do you like this one?" she asked, holding up a necklace.

The prices were not high, and the Indians would bargain, adding to the fun for many passengers seeking souvenirs.

"I have to have it," she said, fingering a single strand of turquoise beads. "Do you think the color matches my eyes?" she asked as she paid the Indian woman.

"Yes," I said, "and the sky, too."

"Aren't you going to buy anything?" she wanted to know. "Did you bring any money?"

I had my stocking of earnings tucked safely inside my old straw valise along with a few things I'd need at the Casteñada. But I didn't tell her.

"All the jewelry is pretty," I said as we headed back to stand with Vi, "but I think I'll save my money."

The three of us were going to Las Vegas on the early train so Vi could visit her mother at the sanitarium on the way. The two chefs, Robert and Gregory, and the kitchen worker, Bertha, would follow later.

My heart raced with excitement when I saw the train down the tracks. We were scheduled to stop at the famous Alvarado Hotel, the Harvey House in Albuquerque.

"We're going to see a movie star," I predicted.

Puffing black smoke and spewing cinders in its path, the train arrived. The ground trembled. I could hardly keep myself from skipping like a little girl across the brick walkway while the passengers disembarked for breakfast.

It was a dream come true. Instead of being inside serving the customers, I was a traveler again. We boarded the train to find a good seat, even though we wouldn't leave for twenty minutes. As we settled side by side onto the plush velvet bench seat, Estevan ran up the aisle to find us. He waved a small envelope, and I thought he was delivering a note to Nellie. For days, she had been getting messages from a special *hombre,* whose name she kept a secret, which was fine with me. I was through with secrets.

But Estevan handed this envelope to me, much to Nellie's disappointment.

"I am sorry, *señorita,*" Estevan said to her, his dark eyes sympathizing with her. "But this night letter is for Clara Massie. The telegrapher said I must deliver it in a hurry. *Es muy importante.*"

I was so surprised that I ripped open the envelope immediately, not noticing that Estevan was waiting and his foot was tapping.

"Estevan works for tips," Nellie reminded me.

"And I am expected in the dining room to clean up," Estevan said. He was proud of being a busboy.

I laid the telegram on the seat, grabbed my straw valise off the overhead rack, and dug around in my money stocking for a dime.

"*Gracias, señorita,*" he said.

Nellie sulked as he ran back down the aisle. With an expression of concern, though, Vi watched as I opened the night letter.

WESTERN UNION
TELEGRAM

RECEIVED AT
BELEN, NEW MEXICO 1920 JAN 18 AM 6 15
WINONA, MISSOURI

MISS CLARA MASSIE
HARVEY HOUSE
BELEN, NEW MEXICO

YOUR SISTER BEULAH ILL WITH TUBERCULOSIS MOTHER AND ALICE REQUESTED I INFORM YOU OF HER WORSENING CONDITION DOCTOR ADAMS FEELS CURE UNLIKELY FAMILY HOPES YOU ARE WELL MISSES YOU GREATLY

MISS ADELE FORESTER

Beulah was dying. I choked back a sob. I had left without even telling her good-bye. Now I was too far away to help my big sister.

I handed the telegram to Vi. She read it quietly and gave me a comforting hug. Then Nellie read it, whispered how sorry she was, and patted me on the arm.

We didn't talk while the passengers boarded the train again. I sat silently weeping, and they both stared straight ahead. It wasn't until we had almost reached the Alvarado that Vi spoke.

"I can arrange for you to take a couple weeks off, and you can go home for a visit."

It was such a nice thing to offer. But I couldn't go home. And I couldn't explain that to someone as good-hearted as Vi. She thought I was an eighteen-year-old woman who had left with her family's blessing, not a fourteen-year-old runaway. So I sat there, not saying anything, not even able to thank her for fear I'd begin sobbing again.

Vi seemed to understand that I didn't want to talk.

"You think about it," she said. "I think you should go, and I can arrange it."

When our train arrived at the Alvarado Hotel, I tried to shake off my feeling of distress. I didn't want to ruin the trip for the others or make Vi wish she had chosen some other girl. I smiled and pretended to perk up by showing interest in the famous resort. It was classy. And romantic. And perhaps the most elegant of all the big Harvey Houses. Some called the hotel the shining jewel in the Santa Fe Railway's crown, the finest railroad hotel anywhere.

I'd heard lots of Harvey Girls and chefs talk about its Spanish mission architecture. Now I was seeing it for myself. It had many arches that led to long, shady porches and balconies overlooking hidden courtyards. Its domed towers could be recognized from miles away. In gray stucco with turquoise trim, it was a mecca for weary desert travelers.

Some came seeking a gourmet meal or an exquisite silver necklace made by Indians and sold in Fred Harvey's Indian building. Others enjoyed a glamorous night at the annual Montezuma Ball. Many came Kodaking, especially to take pictures of movie stars stretching their legs or walking their dogs on the brick walkway before they reboarded trains.

We had just disembarked when word spread among the passengers. "Movie star spotted three tracks over," one person said to another, who relayed it to the next person.

Everyone rushed to get a glimpse.

Nellie started off, but I hesitated, looking at Vi.

"Is it all right?" I asked.

"Sure," she said, "let's see who it is."

I tightened my grip on my valise and ran after Nellie. I was about to see my first movie star in the flesh. And maybe get an autograph. Who would it be? Tom Mix, the cowboy star whose movies were filmed in New Mexico? Or Douglas Fairbanks and Mary Pickford, who had shocked Hollywood by falling in love?

A crowd of excited spectators had gathered around the caboose of a train.

"Come on," Nellie shouted at me, pushing her way through to go right up front.

But I stopped behind the others. Being tall, I could peer over most of their heads.

On the back of the caboose were four German shepherds, two adults and two pups. They were posing for pictures along with a conductor and several other railway men in uniform.

"Where's the movie star?" I asked, not realizing that Vi wasn't beside me.

The man next to me gave me an odd look. Then I heard him tell his son, "He was found in an abandoned German war dog station in a corner of the bunker. His shivering mother and her five pups were rescued by an American corporal."

I laughed, knowing then exactly which famous film star I was seeing. He was Bobby Earl's favorite, Rin-Tin-Tin, the super stunt dog whose trademark was cliff-hanging scenes. I gave up on the idea of getting his autograph.

After that excitement, Vi gave us the choice of staying at the Alvarado for a couple of hours or accompanying her to see her mother a few blocks away.

Nellie chose to stay, and normally I would have, too. But Beulah was suffering the same dread disease as Vi's mother; maybe I could learn something that would help her.

As we walked along the sidewalk, Vi told me why she had brought her mother to Albuquerque.

"It's called the heart of the 'Well Country' because it has opened its arms to lungers from around the world."

I hurried to keep up. Vi could out walk me even though my legs were longer.

"There's no known cure for tuberculosis," she said, "but hundreds of health seekers have come west for climate therapy. Some improve. Many don't."

"Why do they come here?" I asked.

"This is a high desert," she explained. "The altitude is part of the 'cure,' along with dry air and warm sunshine year-round."

We crossed a busy street and headed for a large, stone building, the sanitarium, or sans.

Vi said that for years people didn't think tuberculosis was contagious, but now some knew it was, and children, especially, were susceptible. That threw a scare into me. Alice and Bobby Earl were being exposed to the disease daily.

Vi's mother was in good spirits when we visited her. She was sitting out on the lawn on a chasing chair, a long, low chair with room to stretch out her legs. I shaded my eyes because I still hadn't gotten used to the desert sun.

"I'm chasing the cure," Vi's mother told me after she and Vi talked for a while. "And eating my milk and eggs." She made a face.

Vi explained, "Milk and raw eggs. That's the diet prescribed for lungers."

"I've begged Vi to bring me some real food from the Harvey House, but she says it's against doctor's orders."

Her pale transparent skin reminded me of Beulah's. A terrible fear gripped my heart. I thought Beulah's skin had gotten that way because she stayed indoors so much after her accident. Now I wondered how long she'd had the disease.

Vi's mother coughed and spit many times while we were with her.

But she said she wasn't coughing nearly as much as when she arrived. Then she joked, "I've stopped 'throwing rubies.'"

I didn't know how she could make light of coughing up blood, but I saw that her good humor eased her pain some.

As we walked back to the Alvarado, Vi suggested I tell my folks about the treatment available in New Mexico. Maybe they could arrange for Beulah to come. She said the sans was expensive, but home care was more affordable. Many homes in the area rented rooms to patients for a smaller fee than the sans charged. She could give me the names of some she knew. Vi was being helpful. But it was useless. Where would my mom and dad get the money to spend on climate therapy for Beulah?

The answer popped into my head immediately. I could pay for Beulah's treatment with my earnings. What I had in my stocking wouldn't last long, but I would keep earning more as a Harvey Girl!

18

Caught in a Lie

Hanging across the center arches of the Spanish Mission–style Casteñada, the suffragists' banner read, "Wake Up America."

After we disembarked from the train, we walked to the hotel. I knew that presidents, movie stars, kings, and other famous people had taken the same path. Teddy Roosevelt arrived here year after year for the annual Rough Riders Reunion. Tom Mix, the cowboy star, filmed his Western "flickers" on his own movie lot in the town of Las Vegas. I squinted in the bright sun and looked over my shoulder, scanning the dry plains of northeastern New Mexico. Just like in the Western movies!

And the day before, Carrie Chapman Catt and her army of voteless women had arrived. They were touring the West, meeting with women's groups, governors, and legislators. I'd read all about it in a newspaper I bought at the Alvarado's newsstand. Victory was in sight, as Miss Forester had predicted. But the hard-fought battle would not be over until thirty-six states ratified the Nineteenth Amendment. At least a dozen more were needed.

How my life had changed! I thought about the Ozarks and the life I'd left behind in the shadow of those piney hills. Back then, famous people were merely names I'd heard from Miss Forester. Now I was about to serve a dinner to the courageous suffragists my teacher had told me about.

Nellie and I followed Vi into the hotel lobby and waited while she asked at the check-in desk about our rooms. The dormitory for Harvey Girls, she was told, was in another building across the street.

We set out again with keys in hand, this time passing several groups of sophisticated-looking women. None wore white dresses with yellow sashes or carried yellow parasols the way I'd heard they did at conventions. But they were fancy, well-spoken women. I was sure they were suffragists.

We changed into our clean uniforms, which had been delivered earlier, and reported to the dining room. The suffragists' dinner would begin promptly at eight, and we had many chores to finish before it would be time to serve the appetizers.

First, we were to polish the Casteñada's silver service. With a soft cloth, I spread the polish on each piece, and Nellie wiped it off until the silver gleamed. It was a messy chore, and our hands got dirty. We had to be careful not to dirty our uniforms.

"Isn't it beautiful?" Nellie asked in a far-away voice, admiring the reflection of her blue eyes and flaming hair in the coffee pot.

I agreed.

"Robert told me it's really valuable," she said.

Chefs Robert and Gregory along with Bertha, the salad maker, had arrived at the Casteñada on the last train.

"I wonder how much it's worth," I said.

"Two hundred thousand dollars."

That took my breath away. "Who said?"

"Robert."

I handled the pieces more gingerly.

"They must not have any trouble with sneak thieves at this Harvey House," I said.

Nellie bristled. "Why did you bring that up?"

"I was only marveling that the manager trusts us to polish it," I said. "I didn't mean . . ."

She interrupted, "Oh, I think they are used to having it out of their sight. Robert said they loan it out to other Harvey Houses for special dinners."

I wondered when Robert had time to tell her so much. Vi had warned us both about being too friendly with the chefs. I had just finished spreading polish on the last piece when Nellie reached out to take it. Somehow her hand brushed against the tin of polish, tipping it over. Two or three drops leaked onto her pinafore.

"I'll have to change," she said, not nearly as concerned as I would have been.

"Do you want me to finish wiping the polish off the sugar bowl?" I asked.

"No," she said, as she left. "You start on the napkins."

I headed for the bathroom off the kitchen and washed my hands carefully. Then I helped the other girls fold the starched napkins. After a bit, Vi asked me where Nellie had gone. I told her what had happened. She scurried off to oversee the start of the table setting, which would take a while. The Casteñada's dining room was larger than Belen's.

Minutes later, she was back. "All the girls are needed to set the tables,"she said. "Go find Nellie."

I looked everywhere—our room, the bathroom, the lobby, outside on the lawn, and in the kitchen. Perplexed, I even went back to the dining room, thinking she must have slipped past me. But she wasn't there, and Vi was busy, so I set out again, getting more miffed by the second. What a waste of time to be tracking her down!

I rechecked the kitchen. I didn't see Gregory or Robert, but Bertha was cutting stalks of celery and arranging the hearts on a platter.

"Have you seen Nellie?" I asked.

She rolled her eyes and pointed her elbow toward the pantry door.

What was Nellie doing in the panty? I walked over, eased the door open, and stepped in. They wouldn't have heard me if I hadn't gasped. But I never expected to see Robert standing so close to Nellie that a butter knife could not have been passed between their uniforms. In that instant it all made sense. The messages from an admirer. Nellie keeping his name a secret. Nellie always talking about Robert. They jumped apart when they realized I had seen them.

"Vi sent me to find you, Nellie," I said. "It's time to set the tables."

"She *sent* you?" Nellie asked. "How did you know I was here?"

I figured "here" meant in the pantry. And I didn't want to tattle on Bertha.

I said, "I've looked everywhere else. This was the only place left."

"I can't believe she *sent* you."

"You've been gone a long time."

"I have a good reason."

She had no trouble reading my expression.

"No, really, Clara," she said. "But if you don't believe me, ask Robert."

Robert didn't jump at the chance to back her up.

She began to tell it herself. "You see, someone stole the sugar bowl. And I've been looking for it."

"The silver sugar bowl is missing?" I was dumbfounded.

"When I spilled silver polish on my pinafore," she said, "I took the sugar bowl with me to wipe it while I walked over to the room." Quickly, she added, "To save time."

I fidgeted at the promise of a long story. But Nellie plowed on, in no hurry to let me get back to work.

"Before I changed my pinafore, I came back through the kitchen. To wash the polish off my hands," she said.

I tried to hurry her. "Vi's waiting, Nellie."

She ignored me. "After I washed them, I went to our room and changed, then started back to the dining room. I was nearly there when I remembered the sugar bowl. So, naturally, I went back for it, thinking I'd set it beside the sink. But it had disappeared! Robert's been helping me look for it."

Robert nodded.

"I'm sure it will turn up, Nellie," I said, resisting the temptation to ask why they were searching the pantry if she remembered putting it beside the sink. "I'm going back to help set the tables. You should come, too, and tell Vi what happened."

"I can't do that!" she said, in a panicky voice. "I have to keep looking."

The pantry door opened and Vi poked her head in. "Keep looking for what?" she asked.

Maybe it was the panic in Nellie's voice, but a bad feeling overcame me. I'd done nothing wrong. But I knew trouble lay ahead. For me.

Nellie burst into tears. Robert backed into the shelves behind him, knocking over a large jar of bread and butter pickles. It hit the floor, cracking the glass. Mustard seeds floated across the tile on a current of pickle juice.

I wrinkled my nose at the vinegary smell as Nellie told her story to Vi. I wasn't sure where the smell came from, the pickle juice or her story. She went into even more detail than she'd done before, telling how she had checked with the dishwasher, who said that he always paid special attention to the silver. If the sugar bowl had been in the kitchen, he would have noticed. Then she said she had gone back and checked our room, afraid that she had left it there. And then came back to the kitchen. The story dragged on and on.

I protested once with a shake of my head because she blamed me for telling her to take the sugar bowl with her to our room in the first place.

"I didn't," I said. But no one heard me, and the feeling that trouble was fast approaching overcame me again.

Finally, Nellie ended by saying that Robert had asked everyone in the kitchen. No one had seen the sugar bowl. When she burst into tears again, Robert didn't move forward to dry them. He bent down and picked up pieces of broken glass and hunks of sticky pickles.

Vi's aggravation was no secret. And I was glad when she dismissed me to help in the dining room. I guessed she would make Nellie keep searching for that sugar bowl. I hoped it would reappear as mysteriously as it disappeared, like the silver and china had in Belen.

But the silver sugar bowl was still missing when we served the blue point cocktails to the suffragists. I told myself to pay attention to my job and not worry about something that shouldn't concern me. But I couldn't shake off the bad feeling I had. It turned out that I was even busier than I expected. Nellie's eyes were so puffy from crying that Vi sent her to her room. That meant we were short-handed, and I had to do my job and hers, too.

That didn't worry me one bit.

I felt sure of myself, and several of the suffragists complimented me and the other girls on our efficiency. They also said they had worked hard to get the vote for women like us.

One said, "Voting will soon be your right, but never take it for granted."

"Vote in every election," another told me. "And cast your vote wisely."

After we had cleared away the dessert dishes and refilled the coffee cups, I lined up with the other Harvey Girls at the back of the room to hear the speeches.

Even standing on tired feet, I was in awe of the suffragists who spoke. The stories they told made my heart go out to them and at the same time made me swell with pride. They were strong heroines who endured name-calling and attacks on their private and public lives without giving up. With words, not guns, they had fought and nearly *won* a long, hard war.

The last to speak was Carrie Chapman Catt. She proved to be an inspiring orator. The time was nearing, she said, when women could rejoice because the struggle was almost over. Soon we could enjoy the fruits of our hard-earned liberty. She urged us to work within the political party of our choice and join the newly formed League of Women Voters. I applauded and waved Fred Harvey napkins along with everyone else in the dining room as she called us to assume new duties and responsibilities. We gave her a standing ovation after her final words: "This is the woman's hour."

Long after the suffragists had retired for the evening, I basked in the elation brought on by meeting and serving so many heroic women. I considered my new responsibilities, not only the prospect of voting, but also earning money for Beulah's cure. By the time I finished the after-dinner cleanup, collected my tips—more than I'd ever made in one night—and dragged my weary bones up to my room, I'd forgotten all about the missing sugar bowl. But my memory was refreshed quick enough.

Nellie was nowhere in sight, but Vi was waiting for me. She was standing next to the dresser. I sat down on my bed, too tired even to take off my shoes.

"I'm going to come straight to the point," Vi said. "Nellie has accused you of stealing the sugar bowl."

Her words didn't make sense at first. When it hit me that a sneak thief had called me a thief, I felt pure anger.

Vi stared me straight in the face and asked, "Did you take it?"

I found my tongue. "Of course not!"

"She says she left it in this room when she changed her pinafore. And when you came up here looking for her, you stole it." Vi kept her eyes on me, watching my reaction.

"She knows I did no such thing!" I yelled. "Where is she? I want to talk to her."

"I sent her back to Belen on the last train."

"Then we'll settle this tomorrow when we go back."

"You are not going back to Belen, Clara."

"What do you mean?"

"I'm going to have to let you go."

Had I heard her right? "Vi, I didn't steal anything, not the sugar bowl, not . . . not . . . not anything."

The temptation to blurt out all of Nellie's secrets nearly overcame me. But I clamped my jaw shut and closed my eyes to get control. Nellie knew my true age. I couldn't tattle on her.

"I believe you, Clara. I've checked through your things just to be sure, but I do believe you. Still, I have to. . . ." Her voice broke and she looked away before she went on. "I have to fire you."

"What?" My eyes opened wide. My breath came in short spurts. My pulse raced. "Fire me? No, please, Vi. I love being a Harvey Girl. I need this job."

"I've arranged for you to take the train home first thing in the morning."

My throat tightened so that I couldn't swallow, much less speak.

"You're the best Harvey Girl I've ever trained, Clara, but I have to fire you because you're under age."

19

A Prodigal Daughter?

You're the best Harvey Girl I've ever trained. But I have to let you go. Go. . . . Go. . . . Go. Vi's words echoed in my mind throughout that lonely train ride back to the Ozarks. For nearly two days, I slumped on the seat. I had lied to become a Harvey Girl. And gotten fired. I felt physically sick, and Granny 'hite's home remedies wouldn't help me get well.

Along the way, I imagined disembarking and finding a job. But I thought of Beulah and stayed on the train. As I trudged up the lane to the house, I took note of how shabby the place looked. The house was more weather-beaten, the barn more shoddy and run-down.

The first person I saw was Bobby Earl. He was lurking beside the smoke house. He peaked around the corner and I waved, but he pulled back. Before I could call out, Dad stepped out of the barn and shouted, "Bobby Earl, you ain't half-finished your chores."

When Dad saw me, he stopped in his tracks and broke out in a mean laugh. My knees buckled, but I didn't stop walking.

"Well, lookee here," he said. "If it ain't the prodigal daughter! Don't expect no fancy homecoming, like the prodigal son got in the Bible."

I opened my mouth to protest, *I've never squandered a dime of your money.* But a polite Harvey Girl does not talk back. I clamped my jaws shut.

"Didn't fit in with them city folks, did you? I warned you about gettin' above your raisin'."

It was hard, but I forced myself to turn the other cheek.

"I owe you a whipping for runnin' off like you done," he said. "It was pure foolishment."

I hung my head, closed my eyes, and prayed for courage. When I opened them, I saw him grin. I also saw that he was stooped and shorter than I remembered. He looked worn out. *More like worn down.* Farming the rocky hills of the Ozarks was exhausting work for a man who wasn't getting any younger and had no grown sons to share the load.

Scowling, he demanded, "Why'd you come back?"

"To help Beulah."

"You're too late," he muttered and stomped off to the barn.

As soon as Dad entered the barn, Bobby Earl ran off into the woods.

Fighting the urge to cry, I went into the house. Momma was in the kitchen, drying dishes.

"Need help from a well-trained waitress?" I asked, inhaling the heavy smell of boiled turnips and fried fat back.

"Clara!" she cried. She hugged me long and hard, and her thin body shook with sobs. When she let go, we looked each other over. "Living out West done you good," she said.

She had aged years. I hugged her again.

"Do you like being a Harvey Girl?" she asked.

I winced, but didn't let on that anything was wrong. "Momma, I *loved* being a Harvey Girl."

I sat at the table and told her about the exciting life I'd led. As I did, I made up my mind I'd be a Harvey Girl again, even if I had to wait until I was eighteen. I meant to return to kitchens filled with the aroma of savory French dishes, not turnips and lard.

I saw Dad only at meals. Farm work kept him busy. He was just as ornery as ever, giving orders and venting his anger at the least little thing. I took care not to set him off, even pretending to eat what he made Momma put on my plate. Bobby Earl appeared mostly at meals, too. He'd grown an inch and his too tight britches hit him above the ankles. He still took after Dad in both looks and manner. With a dubious frown, he listened to me tell about seeing Rin-Tin-Tin and the cowboys on the cattle drive. Momma told me he did some fishing and trapping with the new neighbor's boy when he wasn't helping with chores. He stayed gone a lot.

Alice was so glad to see me she clung to my skirts. She cherished the Indian bracelet I'd brought her and wore it all day, then tucked it under her pillow at night. But the look of her worried me. She was pale and skinny.

And Beulah—*bless her heart*—was still clinging to life. She gave me a feeble smile and followed me with her eyes. She lay in her bed, propped up against pillows so that she could cough more easily. For the next six weeks, I tended to Beulah's needs, giving Momma a much-needed break.

And I discussed my plans with Momma. She turned out to be an ally and came up with some suggestions. I wasn't surprised that she was in favor of me taking Beulah to Albuquerque for climate therapy. But I hadn't expected her to think she and Alice should go, too. I didn't see how we could manage, but the more we talked, the more I became convinced.

Slowly, Beulah showed signs of responding to the diet of raw eggs, milk, and other good food, which I spoon-fed her. I got her out of bed for a few hours every day. She didn't weigh as much as the trays I'd toted around the Harvey Houses. I lifted her up and put her in her wicker wheelchair. I tucked one of Grandma Massie's quilts close around her and pushed her into the kitchen. There she sat near the wood cookstove. Its heat was the driest in the house, not nearly dry enough, but better than the dampness of the chilly bedroom when it rained. On clear days, I wheeled her in front of a window. But the Missoura sun wasn't potent like the high desert's.

I told her about being a Harvey Girl and serving dinner to Carrie Chapman Catt and her army of suffragists. She hung onto every word as I read the letter I wrote to Miss Forester about the women's inspiring speeches.

Miss Forester had moved back to St. Louis and was engaged to a young doctor. No teacher had yet been found to replace her, so while Beulah convalesced, I schooled Alice in reading, writing, and ciphering. And I told her the old tales I remembered hearing Momma's brothers tell when I was little. Hillfolks call them windies and claim they aren't lies unless you tell them for the truth. Some are about ghosts. The ones I knew were mostly about monsters that live in the Ozarks, like the whistling whompus, a black cat that lures people into the timber, the whiffle-bird that flies backwards so dust won't get in its eyes, and the snawfus, a white deer with antlers of flowering dogwood branches.

Once I caught Bobby Earl eavesdropping. I thought he was snooping so he could tattle to Dad, who would not approve of the schooling. But when Bobby Earl saw that I'd seen him, he came on into the kitchen. I was telling Alice, for the thousandth time, about the snawfus.

Wide-eyed, Bobby Earl finished telling it for me, adding details I'd forgotten. "The snawfus can fly through the timber of a night," he said, "quiet as a hooty owl, 'cept when it hollers." He cupped his hands around his mouth and let out with a long, loud, "Hallyloo-oo-oo!"

"Who told you that?"

"Frank's daddy," he said. "He's the best old windy-spinner I ever knowed."

I allowed that was probably true since men were just naturally better at telling such stories than women. Then I flattered him by saying he'd grow up to be a mighty fine windy-spinner himself. Grinning, he went on outside.

Alice told me that Frank Reed was the boy whose family had moved into the old Chilton place over on Bear Creek. It wasn't far from our place, and Bobby Earl was running with Frank these days. His daddy worked as a hired man because he'd stopped raising mules. The mule market crashed after the World War ended. The army no longer needed our Missoura mules. They were using trucks now. Dad wanted to hire Mr. Reed to help around our place, but there wasn't enough money. My ears perked up at that.

Each week after learning the three R's, I encouraged Alice to make up her own windies. Her favorite was "The Tale of the Sly Ole Opossum Playing Possum." She told how Mr. Bunter, the hunter, treed a possum. Then he shook the tree until the possum fell out "splat!" into the blackberry brambles. And then Mr. Bunter, the hunter, smacked the old possum upside the head with the limb of a pawpaw. He thought it was dead. He laid it on the woodpile, and when he went back to skin it, it was gone. The sneaky old possum had "woke up" and tiptoed into the pineywoods when Mr. Bunter wasn't watching. The cute way she told it was what made it funny.

I set Alice to counting my savings in secret. I had to know how long my money would last until I could find another job. If I couldn't work as a Harvey Girl, I could try another eatery. Or a sanitarium or a factory or a dime store, though those jobs all paid less. Or I could be a motorette on a streetcar in Albuquerque.

After I wrote to Miss Forester, I wrote two more letters. One to a woman named Anita Chavez that Vi told me about in Albuquerque. Another to Bertha. Bertha's answer arrived first.

> Dear Clara,
> No, the silver sugar bowl has never been found. Yes, Nellie is still a Harvey Girl. She's working at the Alvarado now. Vi got fed up with Mr. Phillips and transferred to El Tovar. You should visit her. You were always saying you wanted to see the Grand Canyon. Alkali Jack says the railroad crews don't miss you at all because the new girl at the lunch counter screams even louder than you did when they hide horny toads under the cups. Ha! Ha!
> Love, Bertha

The morning after the letter from Anita Chavez arrived, I helped Momma fix breakfast. As soon as everybody finished eating, I took a deep breath. I couldn't stop my heart from racing, but I gripped the edge of the table to steady my trembling hands.

I announced, "I'm going back out West. And I'm taking Beulah with me."

Dad's eyes bugged out, and he yelled, "You'll do no such a thing. Beulah's not going anywheres."

"Beulah," I asked, "would you like me to take you out West?" I had told her about the treatments lungers were getting there.

She whispered, "Yes."

"You put her up to answering like that," Dad said.

"Listen to my reasons, please, Dad," I begged. "I've seen people being cured of tuberculosis in the desert. The dry heat, the sunshine, and the altitude can help Beulah."

"Dr. Adams said that, too, Henry." Momma's words were encouraging to me, but they fueled Dad's anger.

"You keep out of this, Wilma," he said. "I'm the head of this family."

Boldly, I explained our plans. "I have enough money saved," I said, "to rent a place for three months. And there's room for Momma and Alice to come, too. Dad, you and Bobby Earl can stay here, tending to the farm until Beulah's well enough to come home." Before Dad could get a word in, I added, "I even have enough money for you to pay a hired man."

Momma agreed. "It's a good idea, Henry. You could hire Mr. Reed. He's a good man. You said so yourself. I talked to his wife at Sunday school, and she agreed to come by and do some of the cooking and cleaning. She can look after Bobby Earl. Her son, Frank, is the same age. . . . "

Dad interrupted. "Nobody's going nowhere. Least of all you, Wilma. It's bad enough that Clara got above her raisin'. But a wife, too! I won't have it!"

"We will go, Dad," I said firmly.

Then Momma spoke again in a strong, determined voice. "Yes, we will go, Henry, because Beulah deserves the chance to get better."

The defeated look on Dad's face made me think he'd given in.

Alice yelled, "Yippee!" She jumped up. "I'll pack."

Before I could tell her Momma had already packed, Dad ordered her to sit down, and she slumped in her seat. Next he ordered Bobby Earl to make sure his leather strap was hanging in the barn. Bobby Earl obliged, but I sensed he mainly wanted to get out of Dad's way.

Dad got to his feet. "You still got a whipping coming, Clara Fern."

I thought of the courage of the suffragists I'd met at the Casteñada as they fought for women's rights. I needed to be strong. I had to win this battle of wits and show my dad a better way, not for myself alone, but for my sisters, too. I held my head high and rose to my full height. I said, "I'm too old to whip, Dad."

"I can still whip Alice," he announced. He grabbed her and took her out of the house. I could hear her whimpering all the way across the yard. I would stop him before he hurt her, but I knew he had to find his strap. I was sure Bobby Earl hadn't followed his orders and had hightailed it over to the Reeds' house.

"This is our chance to get away," I said to Momma. "You hitch up Old Dan to the wagon, and I'll bring Beulah."

She looked bewildered.

I ran into the bedroom and grabbed my money stocking from under the mattress. I counted out the money Dad would need to pay the hired man for three months and laid it on the kitchen table. I gathered up an armload of quilts, my valise, and the one Momma had packed for herself and my sisters. When I got back to the kitchen, Momma hadn't moved.

"We have to hurry, Momma."

I told her again to get the horse. She muttered, "It's the only chance for Beulah. He won't change his mind even if we wait." And she went outside.

I piled the quilts and valises on Beulah's lap and pushed her out. The wheels of the chair bumped across the dirt. I threw the valises and quilts onto the wagon bed, lifted Beulah, and laid her beneath the top quilt. I placed the money stocking in her good hand and told her to squeeze tight. Then I put her wheelchair in the wagon bed.

Momma was leading Old Dan to the wagon. I ran to the barn to get the harness. Dad had Alice at the other end. The leather cracked. I didn't hear a peep out of Alice. What was she doing? I grabbed the heavy harness and began to drag it outside. Momma was right beside me. At the wagon, she said, "I can do this."

Before I heard a second whiplash, I ran to help Alice. In the last stall, Dad stood with his strap raised. Alice's limp body lay in one corner. I clutched my heart.

He saw me and yelled, "You can take the rest of her licks."

The leather strap came down across my shoulder. It stung a little, but he hadn't hit me hard. In one swift motion, the leather whipped up again, then down, striking my arm and leaving a red mark. Furious, I stepped toward him slowly, deliberately. He stood his ground. He had his back to Alice, and I could see her crawling along the edge of the stall. I jumped to the left. My dad did, too. I jumped again and again, moving him in a circle while Alice escaped.

When I had given her enough time to make it to the wagon, I stopped circling and faced him. He grinned and raised his strap. Before it came down on me again, I charged, grabbed it out of his hand, and threw it against the wall.

In a calm voice, I said, "I'm taking Momma and Alice and Beulah out West."

He fumed and sputtered, but he let me go. I went to help Momma. We had just climbed into the wagon when Dad stumbled out of the barn. He mumbled, "It's out of my hands." His eyes were red-rimmed, and he wiped his cheeks.

"I'm doing the right thing for our children, Henry." Momma's voice was firm.

She lifted the reins, and Old Dan pulled us down the dirt road. Dad stood alone. All the anger I'd felt evaporated. My dad's life was hard, and I hoped the money I'd left would make it a little easier.

A mile from the house, I hugged Alice. "You sure gave me a fright," I said.

She grinned, despite her tear-streaked face. "Clara," she said, "you should have known. I was playing possum."

20

At Rails End

Beulah was delighted when we disembarked at the Alvarado. With her good arm, she pointed at America's sweetheart, Mary Pickford, and her new husband, Douglas Fairbanks, strolling up and down the brick walkway waiting for a train.

"Real live movie stars," Momma said. "Imagine me seeing Mary Pickford in person."

"Go on," I said. "Ask for her autograph."

Other people were lining up for autographs, so I led the way, pushing Beulah's wheelchair. Alice was right behind me, so Momma had to come. As we waited our turn, I opened my valise and found the only paper I had, a copy of the Harvey Girl contract I'd signed in Miss Steel's office. Since it was no longer in effect, it would make a good souvenir after a movie star autographed it.

Miss Pickford was a petite woman, not much taller than Alice. I towered over her. But sitting as she was, Beulah could look her straight in the eye.

Miss Pickford wore a gorgeous coat with a fur collar. With a smile and a flourish, she scrawled her name on the back of my old contract and handed it to her tall, handsome husband. After he signed it, he gave it back to me. We all thanked them, twice.

Then Miss Pickford did a really sweet thing. She patted Beulah on the hand. I was touched. Then the movie stars turned to their next fan. Beulah, Momma, and I were in awe. Alice said she wished she'd seen Rin-Tin-Tin.

The train trip had been long and tiring, especially for Beulah. But after we settled into the furnished rooms I'd rented, she perked up. Each day, she chased the cure. Like Vi's mother and so many other lungers, she sat on a chasing chair in the April sunshine of the high desert. And Momma took over the duty of being her nurse again. I enrolled Alice in the neighborhood school. She said she was "skeered" to go, but she liked the teacher and soon found a friend.

Momma's only worry was that Dad and Bobby Earl needed her. But she could see that Beulah's chances of being cured were better in the West. For the time being, this was where she needed to be. She wrote postal cards to Dad and Bobby Earl as often as she could.

When I was satisfied with the arrangements for my family, I packed the new leather grip I'd bought to replace the old straw valise, put on my new navy *crepe-de-chine* dress, and told Momma not to expect me back for a few days.

I found Nellie working at the Alvarado's fancy coffee shop. I didn't let her see me, though. I hung around the hotel, waiting until that shift ended.

I had time to ponder why she'd betrayed me and also why she was such a sneak thief. The first part of the mystery wasn't so mysterious. She told on me to keep herself out of trouble. But why did she steal? I thought back to the early days of our friendship. On the train west, she told me of her mother's death and how her stepmother had claimed her mother's things, which should have passed to her. She felt they had been stolen from her. Was she trying to make up for their loss by stealing from Fred Harvey? That made little sense to me since stolen things could never be as precious as the heirlooms passed down in her family. And it seemed to be a habit she could not, or would not, break. It was too bad because she had only hurt herself. She was a skilled Harvey Girl and could earn her own way in the world. Why risk losing her job? It was beyond me, and I felt sorry for her. But I had made up my mind to confront her.

When I saw her leave the coffee shop, I followed, keeping her red head in sight as she hurried through the luxurious hotel to her dormitory room. I listened at the door to be sure she was alone. Then I knocked.

She called out, "Come in."

She was standing by the window. Her expression of disbelief gave me little satisfaction.

She recovered quickly and smiled. "Why, Clara, it's so nice to see you again. What brings you here?"

"Unfinished business." I set my grip on the floor.

"Are you looking for a job? I could put in a good word for you with the manager."

My resolve weakened. Could she really help me get a job? I'd like to work at the Alvarado. It was close to Momma and my sisters. But if I let Nellie help me, I'd be right back where I'd been before. Because she knew the secret of my age, she might get me to do things, keep me on the edge of trouble. No, I couldn't let that happen again.

"A good word?" I asked. "And later would you tell him I'm under age?"

"I would tell him what a good Harvey Girl you are."

"And I could tell him what a sneak thief you are, Nellie. And that you have Alvarado china hidden away in that trunk you call a hope chest."

I pointed to it on the floor at the end of the bed.

She turned pale. My bluff was working. "Things didn't work out between me and Robert," she said. "I can't afford to lose my job."

"I couldn't afford to lose mine either."

"I'm truly sorry about that. It just sort of slipped out. I didn't mean to tell your secret."

"How could my age just slip out when Vi was asking you the whereabouts of a certain silver sugar bowl?"

She began to weep.

"There's only one thing that will keep me from telling your little secret, Nellie."

"What?" she asked, her tears already dry.

"Give me the Casteñada's sugar bowl."

Another bluff! But it worked, too.

"Why you greedy girl!" she said in an angry voice.

I was taken aback. But I simply walked over and opened the lid of the trunk.

"No!" she yelled. "Don't go rifling through my things. You can have the old bowl."

She knelt down and dug around among Fred Harvey crystal, china, and linens, more than I had helped her return before. The tarnished bowl was at the bottom.

"You could have polished it," I chided, taking it.

"I'm sick to death of polishing silver," she said. "When I do find the right man and settle down, I don't want to own a single piece of silver. It's too much work."

I hoped that would keep her from stealing any more, but I didn't say so. Still, I couldn't resist leaving her with a bit of advice.

"Nellie, what you earn by your own hard work will be the most satisfying."

I put the valuable bowl in my leather grip and left without a look back. The door slammed as I walked away.

An hour later I boarded a train. Destination: Grand Canyon. That night I treated myself to a room at the beautiful Fray Marcos, a Harvey House in Williams, Arizona. Like a regular tourist, I ate in the dining room, enjoying the sumptuous meal without mentioning to the Harvey Girls that I'd once been one of them. I left a big tip.

The next morning I took the last leg of the journey on the Grand Canyon Line to the South Rim. The train was crowded. The conductor told me it was because the dedication of the Grand Canyon as a National Park would be held that day, April 30, 1920. My heart filled with pride to think I'd arrived on such a historic day.

When the train reached the log depot near the canyon rim about two hours later, I disembarked with the other passengers. The depot sat at the foot of a steep hill, leading to the rim. Carrying my leather grip, I walked up the path, part of the crowd. On top of the hill, I caught sight of a larger log-and-boulder structure, the world-famous Harvey House called El Tovar. It was four stories high. I'd often heard travelers I waited on in Belen say it was the most expensive "log house" in America. Many preferred it to the great resorts of Europe. In addition to its dining room, it boasted one hundred guest rooms, art galleries, a club room, a recreation room, a laundry, and a lounge.

The crowd was in a jovial mood. They were dressed in their finery. Businessmen in suits. Sophisticated ladies in fancy city frocks and their best hats. Ranchers and cowboys and mule-skinners in

Western garb. Navajos and Hopis in ceremonial dress. Santa Fe Railway and Fred Harvey employees in uniforms. And me, a tall girl from the Ozarks, who had gotten above her raising and felt she belonged among these people her dad would call "furriners."

Getting above your raising did not mean going back on it, the way Dad thought it did. I never intended to deny my roots. But I did want a better life than what my Momma had.

Quite a few tourists filed up the steps into El Tovar. Some milled around on the porch of the hotel. Others strolled over to Hopi House, an ancient-looking red stone structure, where Hopis lived and worked, making and selling their jewelry and pottery. For a while, I watched them work their craft. They were highly skilled artisans whose people had lived in America long before my ancestors had arrived. Did that make me the "furriner"?

The crowds around Hopi House thickened, and I moved back. But before I found Vi, I wanted to see what Teddy Roosevelt called "the one great sight that every American should see." I headed for the rim and looked down into the Grand Canyon. I stood still, but I became like one of the ravens, soaring above the mysterious mountain range in rainbow colors more than a mile below. It was more wondrous than I'd imagined. Right here in our very own country was a land as exotic as any I'd studied in the geography book Miss Forester showed me. I gazed at the majestic panorama for many minutes. When I walked away, I was ready for the future.

In the lobby of El Tovar, the dedication ceremony was in progress. A throng of people, perhaps numbering in the hundreds, filled the room. It was impossible to get through them, especially carrying my bag. I slipped around the back edge of the audience and listened. A speaker stood on a balcony right below a huge moose head that was decorating the wall. He told how the Grand Canyon had become the newest of the national parks through an Act of Congress the year before.

Hopi Joe Secakuku was introduced. He spoke in his native language while another speaker translated his words into English. Then a different man announced, "Our Hopi friend and his brothers will now chant a sacred invocation to the Kachina, their gods, that the hopes here expressed may be fulfilled." The lights in the lobby went out, except for a lamp over the Indians who had joined Hopi Joe. The low rumble of a drum accompanied their ancient prayer. When the lights came on again, the final speaker told the crowd that the entertainment would conclude outside as Indians sang and danced around a campfire on the circular drive. I stood back as people moved toward the door. When the crowd thinned, I bucked the flow of bodies and found the dining room.

Vi was across the room, overseeing several Harvey Girls setting tables. She was ordering them as though they were all new and all thumbs. When she spotted me, she came over to give me a big hug. She looked weary.

"Clara, tell me you are here to work," she said. "I could sure use a girl with your skills. I guess I'm getting old. I don't have much patience anymore."

I grinned. "There's nothing I'd like better than to be a Harvey Girl again. But I haven't celebrated any birthdays."

"Oh, that," she said. "It was Mr. Phillips who was strict about that rule. When Nellie told him your true age, he sent a telegram ordering me to fire you. I decided not to argue since the managers in Kansas City would back him up."

"I told a lie to get hired. It came back to haunt me."

"I also thought you needed to go see your family."

"You were right," I assured her. Then I told her all about bringing Beulah west to be cured.

"So you do need a job," she said. "The manager here is a reasonable man. When I tell him you're highly skilled, he'll hire you on the spot. Your age will not be an issue."

I could barely believe my ears.

"You can start right after I find you a uniform."

I chuckled. "Will it fit?" I asked.

"No," she said. "It was made for a tall girl who quit last week. It will be way too long."

"I can hem it," I said.

"Been taking sewing lessons, have you?" she asked.

We both laughed.

I laid my grip on a table and got out the sugar bowl. "I'm returning this, Vi. Send it back to the Casteñada."

A hurt look came over her face.

"What's wrong?" I asked.

She shook her head. "Clara, you swore you didn't steal it, and I trusted you. It took me a long time to convince the manager at the Casteñada it wasn't one of my employees who stole it. Now, here you are returning it. I feel foolish."

I let out a relieved sigh.

"I didn't steal it," I assured her. "I rescued it from the copperhead who did."

Shaking her head sadly, she said, "I trusted her, too."

"Come on, Vi," I said. "Let's find that *tall* uniform. Someone once told me I was the best Harvey Girl she'd ever trained. I'm here to thank her for what she taught me."

21

Trails to Tomorrow

I had been working at El Tovar hotel about a week when I saw Jack Wheeler for the first time.

It had been a hectic morning in the dining room. We were short-handed. Vi had asked for five more Harvey Girls to be assigned to our Harvey House, but they hadn't arrived. Dozens of visitors to the new national park had eaten breakfast early and were scurrying off to view the Grand Canyon. Some had planned horseback rides to the outlooks. Others would ride the horse-drawn coaches on short trips to Hopi or Yavapai Points or take the fifteen-mile round-trip along Hermit Rim Road. One party would be riding mules down Bright Angel Trail into the canyon, and another party was going by automobile to Grand View Point.

All were dressed for tramping the trails in the cool, spring weather. The men were dressed in Western wear, many for the first time, judging by the shine on their boots and the stiffness of their khaki trousers. The women wore stout shoes, divided skirts, and broad-brimmed straw hats they had rented in the hotel. I took note of their clothes because I hoped to take the outings on my days off. I wanted to rent a divided skirt, too.

The breakfast rush was over, and I was picking up my tips from under the plates when I noticed that a blonde lady had left her straw hat hanging on her chair. She had been with the group headed to Grand View Point. Thinking that she needed it to protect her fair skin from the bright Arizona sun, I grabbed it, asked one of the other girls to cover my station, and hurried to the lobby. The lady wasn't among the groups there.

Out on the front porch of the hotel, I found her with her party ready to get into one of the sightseeing cars parked in the circular drive. Their tour guide for the outing was introducing himself. I listened, waiting for a chance to give the hat to the lady.

"My name's Jack Wheeler, and I'm from Texas," he said in a drawl I immediately found to my liking. "I'll be your driver today." He tipped his cowboy hat and grinned.

Jack was lanky and probably six feet tall, definitely taller than me. His hair was light brown; his skin was brown, too, from being outdoors a lot. I wasn't close enough to see the color of his eyes. As soon as that thought crowded into my mind, I remembered that it was against the rules for Harvey Girls to date other Fred Harvey employees. That included chefs and managers and the drivers of the sightseeing cars. I vowed to keep my distance. I couldn't afford to lose another Harvey Girl job.

With his hat secured on his head once more, Jack continued talking. His words showed he had some education under his heavy silver belt buckle.

"Ladies and gents, our round-trip will take us twenty-six miles through some of the tallest pines of the Tusayan Forest," he said. "Traveling via Long Jim Canyon and Thor's Hammer, we'll stop at several outlooks and finally at Grand View Point to see the part of the canyon from Bright Angel Creek to Marble Canyon. My favorite sight, which I'll point out along with various other landmarks, is the great bend of the Colorado, the mighty river that chiseled out granite to create the colorful 'big gully' you've come to view. And view you will, since the weatherman has favored us with clear skies. No rainstorms veil the canyon in fog too thick to peer through on this glorious day."

As the visitors climbed into the car, a lady asked about Hopi House, which stood not far away on the brink of the canyon. "How old is that ancient red dwelling?"

Just as curious as she, I listened for Jack's answer. What he said surprised the curious lady and me, too. "Only as old as El Tovar. Both opened in 1905. El Tovar hotel was designed by Charles Whittlesey and cost $250,000. Hopi House, which is a reproduction of the dwellings of the Hopi Indians, was designed by Mary Elizabeth Jane Colter, who is Fred Harvey's chief architect and decorator."

I wasn't sure which stunned me more, that Hopi House wasn't nearly as old as it looked or that a woman had designed it. I wondered what my dad would make of that! A woman being an architect, doing a man's work!

I stood there with my mouth gaping open. It was Jack who noticed me while the party climbed into the car.

"May I be of help?" he asked.

The color of his eyes brought me to my senses. They were blue, the same as the blue plaid shirt he wore.

"Oh, y-y-yes," I stammered. "This hat belongs to the blonde lady. She left it at my station in the dining room."

"Always happy to assist a Harvey Girl," he said, taking the hat and handing it to the lady.

I ran into the hotel, not daring to glance back and glad that those blue eyes were headed in the opposite direction.

In the days that followed, I didn't look for Jack Wheeler. But I saw him once or twice a day, even though there were several hundred people living and working on the South Rim, not counting the sightseers, who numbered about fifty thousand a year. He always tipped his hat and smiled. I nodded, but didn't smile. I couldn't afford to encourage him to think, even for a moment, that I wanted to make his acquaintance.

One morning I passed him when I walked to El Tovar from my room in the girls' dormitory in Bright Angel Camp. The boys' dormitory was on the other side of Grand Canyon village, and we were not anywhere near the stone garage where cars were parked or repaired, so I didn't know why Jack was on the path through the cabins that early. When he spoke, I noticed that his eyes were gray, like the gray coat he was wearing. I barely managed to mumble "Good morning" before I hurried to catch up with the Harvey Girls ahead of me.

Another time, I caught sight of him bent over the open hood of a sightseeing car. He and another driver were fixing the stalled vehicle in the circular drive.

Late on a weeknight, I was working the dinner shift when he and four other drivers sat in my section of the dining room. I took their orders and served their food, the way I would with any customers.

Jack Wheeler was not one of the Fred Harvey bigwigs or Santa Fe Railway officials or anyone special, I reminded myself when my hands shook in an unusual way. I served all diners as if they were aristocrats. I was polite. So was he. I had to smile then, of course. That's what a well-trained Harvey Girl does. The only time I paid attention to the diners' conversation was when the men were requesting more coffee and ordering dessert. After Jack ordered both our fresh peach shortcake and a chocolate éclair, one of the men asked him where he was from.

"I grew up in Harvey Houses in Texas. Gainesville and Slaton to be exact," he answered.

"A Harvey House is an unusual place for a child to be reared," the man said.

I'd been thinking the same thing as I filled their cups with fresh hot coffee and checked the level of cream in the pitcher.

"My dad was the manager. We lived in rooms on the second floor," Jack explained. "My mother helped out in the gift shop when she wasn't schooling me. She'd been a teacher before she married."

"So it was no surprise to your folks that you went to work for Fred Harvey," the man said.

"I've been around Harvey Girls and railroad men all my life," Jack said. He smiled in my direction, and I saw that his eyes were green, the same shade as the forest green shirt he wore. I nearly sloshed the coffee onto the linen tablecloth. "A Harvey Girl taught me to roller skate in the storage basement of the Slaton Harvey House when I was ten," he went on, "and I spent hours talking to the machinists who repaired engines in the roundhouse when I was twelve and up."

Then the other driver began to talk about his own upbringing, and I stopped listening to serve the desserts, after I steadied my hands. I had no way of knowing if Jack or the others had noticed my nervousness, but after they left, I found a fifty-cent piece under Jack's dessert plate. The others all left the usual dime.

On my next day off, I planned to ride a mule down into the canyon. Quietly, because I didn't want to wake my roommate, I put on my rented divided skirt and my stout shoes, then carried my broad-brimmed hat outside. That's when I saw that two inches of snow had fallen during the night, not at all unusual for May. I walked in the direction of the Bright Angel trailhead, not far away, realizing that the snow would extend only a short way into the canyon. There would be summer weather below.

But the closer I got to the trailhead, the more I realized I was in no mood to climb aboard a mule. Some of the ladies who had ridden mules down the dusty, steep, zigzag trails came back complaining that those sure-footed, stubborn beasts were also uncomfortable. I knew that for a fact and thought it amusing that mules were a common sight at the canyon. I'd sent Bobby Earl and Dad a postal card, showing the mules and the guides who led them down the trails. Life on the rim, especially at El Tovar, with its elegant dining room that seated more than one hundred fifty, its own china pattern of white with blue trim, its solarium, music room, and garden on the roof, was glamorous. But there was nothing glamorous about being astride a mule all day, nor trying to walk after you got off the beast.

Still, I yearned to see down into the canyon that day. So I wandered into the Lookout, a small structure on the rim, made of light-colored stones taken from the very spot upon which it was built. My roommate had told me that, like Hopi House, it had been designed by the Fred Harvey architect, Mary Colter.

It made an ideal observatory since it provided a panoramic view of the canyon. I considered it a retreat of sorts, a place where I could sit by the fireplace, enjoy the sight and scent of piñon logs burning, and study a book borrowed from its library. I had already learned a lot about the Grand Canyon from the geology books shelved there. On that day, though, my destination was the tower where I could view the vast canyon through the powerful telescope. In the morning sunlight, I looked at the mysterious shadows, the tops of mountains, the river channel in the center, and the layers of colorful rock formations. From light buff, or Kaibab limestone, at the rim, to gray sandstone to bright red to Redwall, or "blue" limestone, down to grayish green limestone to . . .

That's what I was looking at when Jack Wheeler interrupted my reverie. "The canyon never looks the same twice, does it? It changes with the light."

Startled, I stepped back to look into his eyes. "Just like your eyes," I said. "They change with the color shirt you're wearing. Today, they are green again."

He grinned shyly. "I thought you hadn't noticed me."

"I can't afford to," I told him. "It's against the rules for Harvey employees to socialize."

He seemed relieved. "So that's why you haven't stopped to chat when I've practically made a fool of myself following you around."

"Following me . . ." I repeated. "Is that why you were outside the girls' dormitory early one morning?"

He laughed, then explained. "It's okay for us to get better acquainted. The Harvey rules have always been relaxed here at the canyon. Didn't you notice?"

"I guess so," I told him. "Men don't have to wear jackets in the dining room." Realizing it was time to admit the truth, I went on, "And the manager broke a rule when he hired me. I'm only fourteen."

That's when he really laughed. "I have a confession to make, too. I'm only eighteen, which makes us the perfect ages to become good friends."

There was nothing left for me to do except agree. We headed off to enjoy each other's company over breakfast and to spend our day off together, exploring the rim of the Grand Canyon. Life couldn't get any better for a runaway, who had gotten above her raisin' to become a Harvey Girl and live the American dream.

About the Real Harvey Girls

Be a Waitress! See the West!

A mannequin wearing a Harvey Girl uniform welcomes visitors into her "dormitory room," a popular exhibit in the Harvey House Museum, Belen, New Mexico.
Photo courtesy of the author.

Wanted—young women, 18 to 30 years of age, of good moral character, attractive and intelligent, as waitresses in Harvey Eating Houses.

It's a job that hundreds of young women wanted. Starting in the late 1890s, girls, some as young as fourteen, answered the Harvey Company's ads and left home to work at Harvey Houses along the Atchison, Topeka, and Santa Fe Railway.

Harvey Houses were restaurants started by Fred Harvey, a traveling businessman tired of eating greasy meals served by surly "hash house" cooks in filthy trackside "beaneries." Harvey opened his first dining room in Topeka, Kansas, in 1876. At the company's peak, "Meals by Fred Harvey"—fresh shrimp cocktails, prime rib, French pastries, and many other delicacies—were served to customers in nearly one hundred eating houses from Kansas west to California and south to Mexico.

Fred Harvey was a meticulous manager, always improving the service in his dining rooms. His most popular improvement was the Harvey Girl. After a crew of drunk and disorderly waiters all but wrecked one of his restaurants, he advertised for young women of "good moral character." Most of the girls came from farms in the Midwest. They signed contracts, agreed not to marry for six, nine, or twelve months, and began their arduous training, which many claimed was worse than being in the army.

A headwaitress taught them the "Harvey way." They learned to work in nunlike uniforms, long-sleeved black dresses hemmed exactly eight inches off the floor and covered by a starched white pinafore; to set tables with linen, silver, crystal, and china; and to serve elegant, but *fast*, food to the passengers and crews of trains that stopped for a twenty-minute meal break three or four times daily.

After training, the girls went "out on the line" to a Harvey House. They might find themselves in Sweetwater, Texas; Guthrie, Oklahoma; Albuquerque, New Mexico; Needles, California; or on the rim of the Grand Canyon in Arizona at El Tovar or Bright Angel Lodge, two Harvey Houses you can still visit. The girls earned a monthly wage of $17.50 plus room and board, lived in dormitory-style rooms above the restaurant, followed a strict code of conduct, and (usually) obeyed the curfew to be in their rooms by ten or eleven at night.

The Harvey Girls became famous. Songs and poems lifted them to legendary status. A 1946 Hollywood musical titled *The Harvey Girls*, starring Judy Garland and Angela Lansbury, glamorized them as nice girls who traded the boredom of the farm for an exciting life beside the Santa Fe Railway.

Along with the steam-driven passenger trains that once stopped at bustling railway centers in the "wild and woolly West," the Harvey Girls have drifted into American history. Their proper training, efficient service, and precise manners popularized them as "the women who civilized the West."

Written by Sheila Wood Foard, "Be a Waitress! See the West!" was originally published in Cricket *magazine, February 2000.*

A Note from Sheila Wood Foard

Sheila Wood Foard traveled the Southwest to research the Harvey Girl story.
Photo by Bob Foard.

Harvey Girls were a familiar sight to train travelers across the Southwest from the late 1800s through the first half of the twentieth century. There were nearly one hundred Harvey Houses and an estimated one hundred thousand Harvey Girls.

Yet many people have never heard of the Harvey Girls. I had not until I moved from my home state of West Virginia to New Mexico and read a magazine article about the Harvey Girls. I immediately became fascinated. Here was a little-known segment of women's history. Here was the story of ordinary girls, like me, who had done the extraordinary by leaving home to work, in a day and time when most nice girls didn't hold jobs outside the home, much less go halfway across the country to do so. Curiously enough, these Harvey Girls were paid a good salary to serve meals, to do "women's work." They earned independence because they were skilled, hard-working, poised young ladies.

To learn their history, I collected many articles about Fred Harvey, Harvey Houses, and Harvey Girls. I especially enjoyed reading interviews with former Harvey Girls, who told about their experiences serving gourmet meals to the passengers of the Atchison, Topeka, and

Santa Fe Railway. When Lesley Poling-Kempes' history, *The Harvey Girls: Women Who Opened the West*, was published in 1989, I bought a copy, which I have read, reread, dog-eared, highlighted, and cherished as the bible about Harvey Girls.

While I lived in the Southwest, I visited many of the Harvey Houses, which are still standing, including La Fonda in Santa Fe (now a hotel and restaurant open to the public), La Casteñada (Las Vegas, New Mexico—closed), Gran Quivira (Clovis, New Mexico—closed), and the Harvey House in Slaton, Texas, which has been restored, as have other Harvey Houses, including Casa del Desierto in Barstow, California. I stood on the vacant grounds where El Ortiz (Lamy, New Mexico), the Vaughn Harvey House (Vaughn, New Mexico), the San Marcial Harvey House (San Marcial, New Mexico), and the Alvarado (Albuquerque, New Mexico) once welcomed hungry train passengers. (The Alvarado was demolished in 1969. A paved parking lot took its place. In 2002 the Alvarado Transportation Center, a facility designed in the style of the original Alvarado Hotel, was built on the site of its historic namesake.)

I stayed overnight at the new Fray Marcos, built near the original Fray Marcos, which now houses a small museum, in Williams, Arizona. I traveled by excursion train, the Grand Canyon Railway, to see El Tovar and Bright Angel Lodge. Both of these Harvey Houses are rich in Harvey Girl history and open to the public on the South Rim of the Grand Canyon.

I then toured the restored Kansas City Union Station, where the Fred Harvey Company headquarters were located for decades. Union Station is now a science center and entertainment complex. The original Fred Harvey dining room is a restaurant; the lunchroom is a food court minus the marble counter. Hanging on the wall are huge historic photos, showing Harvey Girls serving meals in the lunchroom in its heyday.

I researched and wrote about La Posada, Mary Colter's masterpiece (now restored) in Winslow, Arizona, for *Cricket* magazine (October 2003). I plan to visit it.

I loved them all. My favorite, however, will always be the Belen Harvey House, which the citizens of Belen, New Mexico, saved from demolition (the fate of many other Harvey Houses). The Belen

Harvey House is listed on the National Register of Historic Buildings and continues to be restored. I served there for three years as a docent in the small first-floor museum, doing research using their archives as well as interviewing other docents who had studied the history of the Harvey Girls, and former Harvey Girls, who dropped by to reminisce.

I have adhered to the basic history of the Harvey Girls as I've told Clara Fern Massie's story. She, of course, lived only in my imagination until *Harvey Girl* rolled out of my printer. But I have tampered with history. I could not resist, feeling it is the right of all writers of historical fiction to take a few liberties with dates and facts. After all, Shakespeare did it even when he wrote his histories.

Here are the places where I stretched things a little:

Rin-Tin-Tin, the super stunt dog movie star did not make his first movie until 1922, two years after *Harvey Girl* takes place. But he did have his photo taken during a layover at the Alvarado. I saw his photo in an exhibit called "Whistle Stop of the Stars" at the Albuquerque Museum in 1996. Also in that exhibit was a photo of Mary Pickford and her husband Douglas Fairbanks, who stopped at the Alvarado on May 29, 1920, slightly over a month later than the day Clara gets Miss Pickford's autograph in *Harvey Girl.*

I do not know if Charlie Chaplin ever sat at the lunch counter in the Kansas City Union Station Harvey House, but I wanted readers to be familiar with the famous comedian so I could tell the story of the gift to Carrie Chapman Catt.

Suffragist Carrie Chapman Catt did not visit the Casteñada during her "Wake Up America" tour, which took place in 1919, instead of 1920, as I state in the novel. But she and other suffragists stopped in New Mexico to convince the legislature in Santa Fe to ratify the Nineteenth Amendment, which they did.

The story about money being donated by the country's school children to buy Carrie Chapman Catt a brooch is based on fact. Many suffragists delighted in telling it at the time. However, it was a young boy who thought he was giving his penny for Charlie Chaplin's cat. In my novel Alice makes the amusing mistake in names.

When I set out to fictionalize the story of a Harvey Girl, I created a main character, who was in many ways typical of all Harvey Girls.

Many of the young women came from farms in the Midwest. I chose the Ozarks as Clara Massie's home because I now live in southern Missouri, a region so similar in landscape and culture to my native state of West Virginia that I feel right at home here.

Like Clara Massie, I can claim hillbilly roots, and I do not feel that "gettin' above your raisin'" means denying your roots. I'm proud of my accent. I grew up listening to hillbilly dialect. I understand such phrases as "gettin' above your raisin'" and "come on in and set a spell." I learned new words when I moved to the Ozarks—jillikens (backwoods), you'uns (y'all, or the plural of you—it is still commonly used in the Ozarks), toad strangler (a downpour of rain, like a gully washer), blinky milk (sour milk), and blue john (skim milk). Vance Randolph and George P. Wilson's *Down in the Holler* was invaluable when I wanted to verify some aspect of Ozark folk speech, which is similar but not exactly the same as the dialect I heard when I was growing up in the Appalachians. I drew on events of my early life in the Mountaineer state and then in the Southwest to write this book, especially on my memories of being teased about my accent. When I needed to know the experiences and folklore of an Ozark native, I read Vance Randolph's books or asked my husband, Bob, who was born in Missouri, not far from the partially fictitious setting of *Harvey Girl*. And I listened to my husband's family tell stories about old-timers, who warned children that Raw Head and Bloody Bones would get them if they misbehaved. Raw Head and Bloody Bones is even scarier to me than the Boogyman that haunted my childhood.

If I could tamper with the history of my own life as easily as I did with historic events when writing *Harvey Girl*, I would go back in time and be a Harvey Girl at El Tovar in 1920 when Clara Massie and her beau, Jack Wheeler, worked there.

My research of the Harvey Girls has not ended with the completion of this book. I remain fascinated by their history as well as with the rest of the story about Fred Harvey and the men and women who worked for him. I will write of them and of the Massie family again.

Passengers wait to board a Santa Fe train in Slaton, Texas. Built in 1912 for $75,000, the Slaton Harvey House (in the background) seated forty-eight customers at a horseshoe-shaped counter. The house has recently undergone restoration.
Photo courtesy of Slaton Railroad Heritage Association.

Harvey Girls and a Harvey House crew of the Slaton Harvey House take a break before the next trainload of passengers arrives. From waitresses and chefs to managers and busboys, Harvey Houses hired many workers. *Photo courtesy of Slaton Railroad Heritage Association.*

Atop an organ in the Harvey House Museum in Belen, New Mexico, is the sheet music of the song from the musical *The Harvey Girls,* "On the Atchison, Topeka and the Santa Fe." *Photo courtesy of the author.*

This formal dining room in El Tovar introduced luxury into the remote Grand Canyon setting. Well-trained Harvey Girls set tables with fine linen, a special pattern of china, sparkling crystal, and gleaming silverware. El Tovar's designer, Charles Whittlesey, created a cross between a Swiss Alpine chalet and a Norwegian villa in what many visitors described as the most expensive log cabin in the United States. *Fred Harvey Photo, circa 1910–1920, courtesy of Grand Canyon National Park Museum Collection.*

Fred Harvey Company touring cars pick up passengers in the circular drive of El Tovar before touring the South Rim of the Grand Canyon. Watching from the roof of Hopi House are Native American employees. Fred Harvey's architect, Mary Jane Colter, designed Hopi House as a re-creation of part of a Hopi village of Old Oraibi. After Hopi House opened in 1905, Hopi craftsmen lived and worked there, making pottery, weaving rugs, and selling arts and crafts to tourists. *Fred Harvey Photo, circa 1922, courtesy of Grand Canyon National Park Museum Collection.*

These visitors view the canyon through a powerful binocular telescope from the telescope tower of Lookout Studio. The small observatory, designed by Mary Jane Colter in 1914, is a primitive-looking structure made of rough-cut Kaibab limestone blocks that appear to have been taken from the canyon rim site upon which it was built. Located on a promontory, "the Lookout," as it was originally known, seems at first glance to be part of the canyon rim, rather than man-made. *Fred Harvey Photo, circa 1915, courtesy of Grand Canyon National Park Museum Collection.*

Before the Grand Canyon became a national park, most of the people living there seasonally or year-round worked for the railroad or for the Harvey Company. This "Fred Harvey Bunch" is comprised of five Harvey Girls and other Harvey employees outside Bright Angel Hotel. The strict Harvey rules against employees socializing were relaxed because the area was so remote. After work or on days off, employees attended dances or parties and hiked or rode mules, horses, carriages, or cars on the trails. *Brown Photo, circa 1915, courtesy of Grand Canyon National Park Museum Collection.*

The station crew lines up in front of Santa Fe Engine 1251, which pulled passenger cars from Williams, Arizona, to Grand Canyon Depot, a rustic structure built in 1909. Although today's visitors can once again ride an excursion train to the historic depot, passengers, eager for a glimpse into the grand gorge, no longer arrive in the middle of the night in Pullman berths. *Kolb Brothers Photo, circa 1915, courtesy of Grand Canyon National Park Museum Collection.*

About the Author

Sheila Wood Foard has been writing children's stories, articles, books, and poems since she retired from teaching creative writing, journalism, and English in Albuquerque, New Mexico. She is now a writing instructor for the Institute of Children's Literature.

Her writing has been published in *Highlights for Children, Cricket, Spider, Ladybug, Cicada, Hopscotch for Girls, Nature Friend, Wee Ones, Skipping Stones, 'TEEN, Missouri Conservationist for Kids,* and other magazines. Her articles for adults have appeared in *ByLine, Country Home, Albuquerque Journal, New Mexico Magazine, New Mexico English Journal,* and other publications, as well as online.

Chelsea House published her biography for teens, *Diego Rivera* (the Mexican muralist), in 2003. She has written press releases, profiles, publicity articles, feature articles, and reading passages for educational testing companies; haiku, sonnets, free verse, and rhyming poems for children; rebus stories for children's magazines and hidden picture activity booklets; brochures for the museum in the historic Harvey House in Belen, New Mexico; and three waysides (signs along hiking trails) detailing the flora, fauna, and CCC history along the Slough Trail near Big Spring in Ozark National Scenic Riverways. She did a fourth wayside about the Civil War in the Ozarks for the park's headquarters. She also designed and wrote a twenty-page Junior Ranger Activities Booklet for the same national park.

POLK COUNTY PUBLIC LIBRARY
31250200045170

President Teddy Roosevelt said the Grand Canyon was "the one great sight every American should see." On March 17, 1911, he led John Hance and the Colgate Party down the dusty switchbacks of Bright Angel Trail. Emery Kolb photographed Roosevelt's outing. The Kolb brothers also filmed and showed the first motion picture of the Grand Canyon—their own perilous river trip down the Colorado River in 1911. Ellsworth and Emery Kolb's photographic studio, which clings precariously to the canyon rim, is now on the National Register of Historic Places. *Photo courtesy of Grand Canyon National Park Museum Collection.*

Outside the public garage at Grand Canyon, drivers pose on a Pierce Arrow touring car. The Fred Harvey Company owned and operated many touring cars, which became popular after good roads were built. Visitors could tour the canyon rim more quickly and in greater comfort in cars. Drivers acted as guides, pointing out prominent sites and answering historical and geological questions. But not all roads were open to cars. Only horse-drawn coaches were permitted on Hermit Rim Road or the road to Yavapai Point. And the only way to reach the canyon floor was on foot, mule, or horseback.

Fred Harvey Photo, circa 1922, courtesy of Grand Canyon National Park Museum Collection.

"A mile deep, miles wide, & painted like a sunset. That's the Grand Canyon of Arizona," states a *Santa Fe Railroad Magazine* advertisement that ran in *Harpers Weekly* in 1910. The illustration depicts a Harvey trail guide speaking to a woman as he points toward the canyon. Ads like this lured thousands of visitors to the park.

Photo Courtesy of Grand Canyon National Park Museum Collection.

For Further Reading

Berke, Arnold. *Mary Colter, Architect of the Southwest*. New York: Princeton Architectural Press, 2002.

Bryant, Keith L. *History of the Atchison, Topeka, and Santa Fe Railway*. New York: Macmillan Publishing Company, 1974.

Foard, Sheila Wood. "An American Original," *Cricket*, October 2003.

Foard, Sheila Wood. "Grace Going Solo" and "Be a Waitress! See the West!" *Cricket*, February 2000.

Foster, George H., and Peter C. Weiglin. *The Harvey House Cookbook*. Atlanta: Longstreet Press, 1992.

Grattan, Virginia. *Mary Colter, Builder Upon the Red Earth*. Flagstaff, AZ: Northland Press, 1980.

Howard, Kathleen L., and Diana F. Pardue. *Inventing the Southwest*. Flagstaff, AZ: Northland Publishing, 1996.

MacNeil, Robert, and William Cran. *Do You Speak American? A Companion to the PBS Television Series*. New York: Doubleday, 2005.

McCrum, Robert, Robert MacNeil, and William Cran. *The Story of English*. New York: Penguin Books, 2002.

Morris, Juddi. *The Harvey Girls: The Women Who Civilized the West*. New York: Walker and Company, 1994.

Poling-Kempes, Leslie. *Far from Home: West by Rail with the Harvey Girls*. Lubbock: Texas Tech University Press, 1994.

Poling-Kempes, Leslie. *The Golden Era: West by Rail with the Harvey Girls*. Lubbock: Texas Tech University Press, 1997.

Poling-Kempes, Leslie. *The Harvey Girls: Women Who Opened the West*. New York: Paragon House, 1989.

Randolph, Vance. *We Always Lie to Strangers: Tall Tales from the Ozarks*. New York: Columbia University Press, 1951.

Randolph, Vance, and George P. Wilson. *Down in the Holler: A Gallery of Ozark Folk Speech*. Norman and London: University of Oklahoma Press, 1953.